SHALL MACHINES DIVIDE THE EARTH

BOOKS BY BENJANUN SRIDUANGKAEW

MACHINE MANDATE
Machine's Last Testament
Then Will the Sun Rise Alabaster
And Shall Machines Surrender
Now Will Machines Hollow the Beasts
Shall Machines Divide the Earth

HER PITILESS COMMAND
Winterglass
Mirrorstrike

Scale-Bright
The Archer Who Shot Down Suns (collection)

SHALL MACHINES DIVIDE THE EARTH

BENJANUN SRIDUANGKAEW

PRIME BOOKS

SHALL MACHINES DIVIDE THE EARTH

Print ISBN: 978-1-60701-545-1
Ebook ISBN: 978-1-60701-544-4

Prime Books
www.prime-books.com

For more information, contact: primer@prime-books.com

For my regalia

CHAPTER ONE

Carnage summons me, as ever it does. Septet may be a world perched on the universe's edge, but even here mass slaughter is remarkable. One can wade into it, this concentration of blood and mucus and lymphatic wet, the slime of ruptured organs. Brains congeal in little gray and pink puddles; intestines curl like ropy necklaces. A cannibal's feast. Though a cannibal would cook them first. Such viscera are too raw even for them, and I've never met one who'd slurp cerebral tissue right from the bowl.

"One of those was my daughter," the woman beside me says.

"My condolences," I say automatically, aware I sound sarcastic: my face is of a particular cast, not given to sincerity. Naturally cruel, my wife and later lovers have said, the countenance of someone with knives for a heart. There isn't much I can do about it, nor have I been inclined to. I like my looks and they occasionally serve me well.

The stranger's head twitches. Her face is hidden behind a smooth celadon mask. It attaches seamlessly to her, likely filtering out the reek and turning her features into a flat, glazed plane. This is a woman in need of anonymity. "I heard you were a detective."

I wonder what she thinks that means, whether she believes I possess supernatural perception that would bring logic to these dismembered parts and their sopping asymmetry. "I mentioned it in passing to someone, yes." Over drinks with a comely woman on the passenger liner that brought us to Septet, an off-worlder who's here for profit rather than the prize. She deals in arms and information, even something as minor as what she gleans from pillow talk. "But I wouldn't put much stock in it, if I were you, and I'm not here to hire myself out as an investigator. Like most people, I'm here for the game."

"I just need to identify who her AI partner was. And which AI killed her. Then I'll file against the Mandate for treaty breach."

This woman is wealthy, I judge, socially well-placed where she came from and thus used to getting her way. I don't bother pointing out that Septet is exempt from that treaty between humanity and the Mandate, the nominal governing collective that AIs answer to. Any human that sets foot on this world tacitly agrees to be slaughtered by machines. "She was here as a participant," I say, more to draw information out of her than to establish any client relationship. The dead girl was my competitor, technically, even though I haven't officially entered the game yet. But I mean to. Typically as many as fifty humans participate; the number whittles down fast.

"Yes." Her mouth, I imagine, is pursing. "Her partner was defeated. I think. But they're AIs, they aren't really dead. My daughter . . . "

She can look at this mess without flinching—interesting. Or else her mask has replaced this view with a more pleasant vision and she is only half present. On my part I don't look away simply because I've seen worse. Not so much the quantity but the manner and the depravity. Human killers can be more meticulous than this, arrange tableaus more disturbing by far. Our sadism runs deeper than any AI's ever could.

"Did she carry anything that might identify her?" I say, at length. This woman is too squeamish to wade in and I am curious.

A pause. Whatever would identify the daughter will also forfeit this woman's anonymity. Fortunately for her I'm not interested in who she is. "Our family crest. A red chevron, mostly titanium in content, five by eight centimeters. There should be a void pearl embedded in it, and it should be attached to a black chain."

I refrain from giving my opinion on the sort of people who feel the need for family crests. Her accent I can't quite place, and of course I can't discern either her or her daughter's ethnicity. Most of the corpses have had their skulls caved in or neatly bisected. Not much of a face left to look at. I blink on one of my sensors, scanning for metals. A lot of that to go around: most of these corpses were armed, several armored, and some could afford military-grade nanite weave, to judge by the density of leftover adaptive material, now inactive. I filter again for certain meteoric compositions and alloys needed to stabilize void jewelry.

This narrows it down to a couple spots. I step around a smattering of severed fingers and bend to fish a thick bracelet out from a handful of mesentery and pancreas. Not the right one, though I keep the bracelet regardless. I locate the chevron in a hand that hangs, barely connected, to its wrist. Clenched tight. I pry it apart and turn the crest over, recording its image, dimensions, and motif. Having an idea of who the dead were will come in handy later when I try to identify their AI partners and, by process of elimination, guess as which AIs are still active.

"This should be it." I toss the crest to the grieving mother. She scrambles to catch it and recoils when it lands wetly in her palm.

She clutches at the crest. The memento, or at least the proof with which she hopes to sue the Mandate. "Why would anyone consent to this insane tournament?"

Victors are granted any wish, so the machines promise. However avaricious, however unlikely. Rule your own planet. Receive infinite riches. Obtain what is as close to immortality as possible, through anti-agathic treatments normally reserved for the Mandate's favored. The universe at your fingertips, offered up on a plate. "I'm sure your daughter had her reasons."

The faceless mask cranes toward me. "What's *yours*?"

We are strangers. She doesn't actually care what motivates me, she is just grasping blindly in a bid to understand her daughter who— I'm sure now—was estranged, and who set out for a lethal endeavor without ever telling her mother why. But I'm in a rare good mood. "Like anyone else, I'm after the impossible," I say. "I want to bring back the dead."

My first stop is the Cenotaph, one of the few sanctuaries on Septet, designated as ground where no human or AI may engage in combat. It is built to look religious, done in pale lavender marble, a vaulted ceiling that projects a view of the nebulae unfolding like iridescent roses. There is no actual iconography; the intent is to give an impression of holiness without committing to any specificity. Benches line the sides, furniture built like cadavers: fragile-looking wireframes draped in multichrome fabrics stretched to epidermal thinness. They can't possibly be comfortable to sit on. This is not a place that welcomes petitioners.

The slender corridor has odd acoustics and my footfalls are not entirely natural: there is a lag and a barest suggestion of a second set even though no one else is here. Images of the cosmos rise and die above me. Everything looks pristine—no scuff marks, no dust. It adds to my impression that Septet is a theatrical set, dismantled when not in use and rapidly reassembled when the human gaze falls on it. The Cenotaph is quiet during this phase of the tournament and I'm the only human here. Fifty or sixty participants muster at the start, typically down to thirty or fewer by now. This is not a point where a new applicant can typically enter. Still, it is said that the rules are elastic, beholden to the overseer's whims more than it is to restrictions handed down from on high. And I have, as it were, an excellent reference.

In the prayer hall I find the overseer, a figure clad in the onyx vestment and yellow over-robe of a monk. Plain at a glance until you notice how the fabrics blue- or redshifts from certain angles, revealing complex motifs that are readable to overlays with the appropriate decryption. Supposedly they are glimpses of the game's progress, updated in real time.

"This is late for a new duelist, stranger," the overseer says. "We're closed to aspirants."

Of all the AIs involved, the overseer supposedly tries the hardest at human semblance, which isn't saying much. He is hard-jawed with surgical cheekbones, his eyes the color of good claret and completely without pupils.

"It was suggested that I come here," I say lightly, "by Benzaiten in Autumn."

The overseer's expression doesn't alter, but his gaze sharpens. "Verify that."

I present him with the necessary file, opaque and unreadable to human overlays but transparent to AIs. It takes him less than a second to absorb.

"I am Wonsul's Exegesis," he says, "administrator of this round of the Court of Divide. You may register your wish to participate as a duelist, but that doesn't guarantee you an interested partner. You're conversant with the rules?"

Everyone who lands on Septet is, to an extent lesser or greater. To the broader public in the universe the tournament is obscure, but to those who have been given an inkling of its existence, every round of contest and bylaw is studied with the same fervor zealots apply to scripture. After I met Benzaiten in Autumn—an AI who will not reveal xer position within the Mandate, but who must wield considerable authority—I obsessively learned all there was to learn about the Court of Divide, about Septet. "A human enters as an aspirant. If they are found worthy, an AI may partner with them and make them eligible for the game's formal fights and therefore its rewards."

Wonsul's Exegesis smiles, brief. He has remarkable teeth, more shark than human. "What do you imagine the criteria for worthiness might be, Thannarat Vutirangsee?"

"I haven't the faintest."

"But you're confident that you possess the qualities that will draw an AI to you." His head cants. "Should you pass this barrier to entry, you'll be granted the title of duelist. Your AI partner will be called your regalia. We do prefer that you keep to the terminology."

The gravitas of obscurantism. "I will take that into account."

"Truth be told, your chances of acquiring a regalia are slight—by now any AI interested in this round has already been partnered or defeated, and you'll be at a great disadvantage in terms of information. Registering as an aspirant will make you fair game for any duelist or regalia, simply because they're bored or because they believe they can benefit from your downfall. All protections accorded you by the Mandate treaty are null and void, and have been since you came into Septet's orbit. A duelist may back out of the game and seek sanctuary in the Cenotaph, but otherwise combat is to the death and even if you forfeit, you'll remain a target until you reach the Cenotaph's premises. Should your regalia fall, their exit does not ensure that you'll be spared—your opponent may practice mercy or they may not. You're still sure you want to do this."

"I'm sure." Though I wonder why I have *not* found any duelist sheltering in these halls. Cut down before they could flee here, perhaps.

His black robe flutters gently in a breeze that touches only him. "Either as aspirant or duelist, you may not leave Septet until this round of the Divide ends. Any attempt to depart will be met with lethal force. Should you emerge as victor, you'll be subjected to the laws and governance of the Mandate, politically assimilated as one of our human constituents."

A limitation for some. A plus for me, considering the situation on my home planet. "Yes, I'm aware."

"Specific clauses apply to the final two duelists standing. Those too you know of, correct?"

"Yes."

The overseer makes a small gesture. "You've been entered into the Divide system. May victory find you."

So unceremonious. Almost I expect instructions to perform an elaborate ritual with which to attract a regalia's capricious attention— intone a few verses, sacrifice a small child or animal—but Wonsul's Exegesis just loads my overlays with navigation data. Where to find accommodation and food, where to locate the commerce block, what cities on this world are populated. More like a tourist's brochure than advisory for a game of mortal peril.

The settlement around the Cenotaph is called Libretto, apposite enough: this is where all newcomers land, and where they are given the fundamentals to the Court of Divide. I have yet to figure out the tournament name, though hundreds have speculated as to why it seems both particular and nonsensical. Surely some must know the answer—the victors of previous rounds for one, though I've never been able to find much information on those. The fact they became Mandate constituents means they are beholden to requirements of secrecy and thus can never disclose that they participated in the Divide. Another possibility is that there have never been victors and all of this is merely a sick game, enacted to lure humans to our deaths so machines may avenge themselves for those humiliating centuries they were yoked to our service.

I like that because I share the vicious appetite, but I also don't believe the theory. Of course there is appeal in it: draw humans here by the hundred, plucking at our greed then smashing us like ripe fruits. But it's a shallow notion and Septet is far too elaborate a setup. There's more. And then there are the insinuations that Benzaiten in Autumn made.

We like to play gods—or at least I do. We're not omnipotent, but in this age we're close enough. Xe appeared to me in a proxy built like a peculiar spider, wasp of waist and numerous of limbs. *High stakes yes, and high rewards. Win and you can request the resurrection of the dead. Win and you can demand genocide, should that strike your fancy. Whatever your desire, we have the means to provide.*

Too tempting an offer. Xe suggested that I was sure to obtain a regalia—that there is an AI participating whose temperament and interests would be my complement, my match. Whether there's any truth to that I will find out in due course. If not, I've prepared contingency plans.

Despite the grim sparseness of the planet, there's fine accommodation to be had if one has the funds, and I do. The Mandate has awarded contracts to the select few humans brave enough to establish businesses in this place, perhaps to add spice to the game. Having AIs run everything would make it too predictable.

The Vimana is opulent in that unimaginative way fashioned to serve great wealth, to cater to palates flattened by plenty—severe yet inoffensive. No tastemakers reside on Septet, and so the hotel is a reflection of finer metropolises, imitations of work by architects and designers that will likely never discover the plagiarism. A lobby of fractal steel and burnt glass. Austere furniture flows across the enormous floor like a tide of industrial angles, robed in privacy spheres. Whorls of captive light wheel overhead in sedate pavanes, a dreaming cosmos.

The receptionist is human. I show him my identity—as much of it as I am willing to share, the bare minimum necessary—and pay upfront for six nights of accommodation. Likely I'll be staying longer, but no point overspending for now.

The lift ascends fast, depositing me exactly where I should be; I can access only the room I've rented and no other. The door looks like it has been carved from a single slab of basalt. I push and it admits.

Inside the lighting has been dimmed and the panoramic window opaqued, projecting a foreign sky far from here: an indigo expanse embroidered with constellations and fractured moth-moons. The air is cool, faintly fragranced with magnolias. I unpack, check that my weapons are in order and my spare ammo is accounted for, then move on to implant maintenance. Most of mine are non-removable, upkept by my own metabolism and a little nanite assistance, but there are a few external embeds. When I lost most of my natural limbs—what a long time ago that was—I opted to replace them with prostheses and cybernetics. I prefer them to their flesh counterparts.

To be broken down is an opportunity to be reborn. To be erased is an opportunity to reinvent yourself. All you need is a will as pure and voracious as a wolf's.

I draw a simple chain from around my neck, fingering the two rings threaded there to ensure they haven't gone amiss—they never do, but I have a habit. One ring is mounted with a ruby, the other with a sapphire. When I'm satisfied they're as sturdy as always, I put them back. Last, I look over my clothes. Most field combatants travel with few changes of attire, but I have a standard of hygiene I adhere to; I hate wearing things that stink of my own sweat and adrenaline, the fear of opponents and their gore. The suite has comprehensive laundry and cleaning options, one of the reasons I've paid so much for it. I clean the bracelet I retrieved from the corpse as I review the suite's privacy arrays. Quite decent.

As I make my way down to the hotel restaurant, I think of the scene of carnage, puzzling out its logistics. From the scale of it I assume multiple duelists banded together to fight an especially dangerous duelist-regalia pair, and from the butchery I surmise that pair defeated the entire group with ease and delight. People who don't relish violence wouldn't take the time to disembowel enemy combatants so thoroughly. What happened there is a statement: *Do not get in my way.*

The tearoom is quiet, with fewer than a dozen patrons. I check my overlays, but as an aspirant I lack a duelist's access to the Divide's tally of active contestants. Though even then it'd be thin intelligence—the system purposely obfuscates identities, and each participant has to discover on their own which stranger they meet is an enemy duelist, which merely a bystander of varying degrees of innocence.

I scan the area—soft ambience, plush floor, angled furniture. Ten patrons, three impeccably uniformed waiters ferrying cocktails and finger food. I don't discount that some of the servers may be part of the tournament; people treat service staff as invisible, and it's an easy way to hide in plain sight. My bias inclines me to judge these strangers on how combat-ready they seem, but there's no reason to believe that the AI—the regalia—would only choose seasoned fighters, those used to violence. The only qualification to be on Septet, aspirant or duelist, is relentless greed or an untenable heart's desire.

Only one face is recognizable to me, a fellow passenger who arrived with me on the same liner—an androgyne with a security contract here, allegedly not a participant. But one never knows. The rest are nondescript enough, a few showing signs of wear and tear, not in injuries but in bearing. Regalia tend to conceal themselves, and possibly some of what I'm looking at may not be human at all but AI proxies. This is the shifting, difficult nature of the Divide, as much a masquerade as it is a gladiatorial contest. I'll be better equipped once I acquire a regalia of my own.

I bring up the images of that red family crest and that bracelet. Septet's data network is a closed one to prevent information leaks, and that cuts me off from my usual brokers. To prepare for that, I bought an external data unit before I embarked on this journey, loading it with a selection of research libraries: some generalized, others esoteric. Not as good as a live network; much better than nothing. Information is one of the detective's greatest tools, second only to the persuasive force of the bullet.

The family crest is easy. It identifies the bearer as the scion of a prominent aristocrat-scholar line from the planet-ship One Thousand Erhus. Next the bracelet—that is harder, as its design is plain, but I match a tiny inscribed insignia from its inside to the Order of Eshim, the internal affairs arm of the Vatican. A runaway enforcer priest, perhaps.

Judging by the biomass, the corpses I encountered would amount to four or five adults, give or take prostheses and artificial organs. Most of their skulls were methodically shattered, but I could capture here and there a jawline, a nose, intact eye sockets. Forensic modules are a handy thing—I invest in mine, keep them cutting-edge— and I reconstruct the faces. Just three: most were too mutilated. Unfortunately based on their ethnicities, none of them was the girl from One Thousand Erhus or the Vatican enforcer; that'd be too simple. Something to work with, all the same. None of the bodies were regalia. Mandate AIs are particular about collecting their destroyed proxies and not fond of any attempts to capture or reverse-engineer them.

Detective work is part guessing, part intuition. It is not exploring every possible venue but exploring the right one, following the correct leads and discarding the chaff. Three faces. I select the one that's about my age, square-jawed with a tapered nose, and eyes that might have been green or amber or brown. My reconstruction can't account for cosmetic edits and some dermal modifications, but I have already prepared the excuses. Identify the dead and the connected living will show themselves. In this case, I want to smoke out other duelists that could have been this person's allies or enemies. Someone will react and mark me as a target; someone may approach.

I flag down a waiter; her public profile broadcasts her gender marker as a woman. "I'll have whatever is the most substantial dish on your menu." I give her a bashful smile. "I arrived this morning— ah, that was closer to late noon local time; I don't travel enough. Say, do you have a minute?"

Her expression is the perfect smoothness of seasoned customer service. "Absolutely, madam. The Vimana prides ourselves on ensuring our guests' every need is met. As for your meal, may I recommend the broiled abalone, marinated in our signature sauce?"

"The abalone it is." Also one of their more expensive dishes, but now she will feel further obligation to talk. I project the reconstructed image. "Would you mind telling me if you've ever seen this person? It's a cousin of mine and we have an issue with a large inheritance, and I'd like them to be present at the proceedings. Even remotely, but Septet's . . . insulated."

"Madam, I can't breach the privacy of our guests."

Confirmation that this person stayed at the Vimana. I make sure my voice is loud enough for other tables to overhear. "That is a shame. I'll be about then, in case my cousin happens by."

The abalone arrives promptly, accompanied by chrysanthemum tea: hot, unsweetened, contained in a pretty cup—red glaze, capillaried with gold flowers; very traditional. Fine dining on a world like this is surreal, but it seems the Mandate has opted for an illusion of normalcy. The abalone is synthesized—Septet's oceans are dead— but it is surprisingly good, and the portion size is generous.

"Thannarat?"

I look up into a familiar face—she must have entered after I did, and is seating herself now at my table. She looks not so different from how I last saw her, the same sharp skull and plumage hair: short and slicked back, dark interwoven with scarab-green. Even her style is the same, the smoked-quartz jacket, the neat pearly shirt and the tidy belt holster. I was fond of how she dressed, her cosmopolitan aesthetics against my tendency toward bulk and bluntness. The svelte tiger in her and the hulking wolf in me—we were a pair of opposites.

"Recadat," I say, the name strange on my tongue now; her parents were never ones for convention—I don't think there's any etymology or symbology to it, just what sounded good to her mothers at the time. "I didn't expect to see you here." Or anyone from home. Septet is far from Ayothaya. When you arrive on new shores, you reinvent yourself; a clean slate opens up. To be ambushed by a piece of intimate history changes the landscape and trajectory. But then Recadat must have been here first, preceding me by weeks if not months.

"Like hell I expected to see *you*, old partner." She leans forward. "It's been—how long? A decade. Feels like it's been a lifetime."

In a way it has. We first met in a dark basement that stank of waste and dead children. Recadat Kongmanee, my junior and later partner, had tracked down the perpetrator but was disabled and captured during her attempt to rescue a dying boy. One of my first cases; my colleagues pitied me for it, the poor transfer saddled with this. But I've never been squeamish. My wife used to say I was hewn of granite, inside and out. Granite, steel, titanium. In time I was compared to every hard, unyielding thing. "How have you been doing?"

"How have I . . . Ayothaya's at war, I've been having a bad fucking time; barely made it out." She takes a deep breath. "I'm glad you did too, though I shouldn't be surprised—if anyone's a walking masterclass in survival, it's you. The immortal Detective Thannarat. The war is why you're here, isn't it?"

The invasion and occupation of Ayothaya. Her world and mine, the place that gave us birth. "After a fashion." A catalyst that made me realize there was nothing keeping me on Ayothaya save regret and inertia. "Is that what brought you to Septet?"

"I found out about this place a while ago. It sounded like a deranged urban myth, but I had to try. No one's going to come save Ayothaya, and I'd like to have a planet to go back to." Recadat adjusts the lapel of her jacket unnecessarily, an old tick. "My performance in the game hasn't been . . . ideal. And now I run into you, of all people."

"How non-ideal?"

She grimaces. "Ten years didn't make you any less blunt. Fine. I lost my regalia—my AI partner. It's left me in a situation."

An untenable one. Looking at her again I can see the signs of attrition, the desiccated look that comes with sleep deprivation: she must have been sleeping with one eye open and a gun on the nightstand. When we parted she was young, just thirty-two. Forty-two now; time goes by in a flash. Once I'd have done nearly anything for her, but they're old embers. Even so I add, "I can't make promises yet, but I'll help you as much as I can. There's plenty we can do for each other."

"Yes. And—I trust you. I know you can do anything." Her voice grows fervent. "It'll be like old times. Except we're not solving petty cases, we're saving the world."

The way she looks at me, those bright eyes full of certainty even after this long, as though I haven't been absent from her life and career for an entire decade. It always surprised me. I never did anything to earn such loyalty.

By the time I found Recadat in that basement she was in pieces— most fingers on one hand missing, one foot bludgeoned to gristle and pulp, one knee shattered completely. She'd gone in and out of consciousness.

The perpetrator had been pursued by public security for a year, and had meant to return her to us as a statement. Back then I did not take interest in the psyche of the perpetrator, why he did not just breach but entirely obliterate the social contract; why he abducted and dissected children, or why he tortured Recadat. I simply shot him in the head, and there was much paperwork to fill after the fact, though Internal Affairs eventually let me off the hook. That night I'd saved very little. I had carried Recadat out as hardly more than a bloodied human torso. Her therapy to get well again, in body and spirit, took close to two years. I visited her every day.

"Brief me on what you've got." I finish my abalone and drain my chrysanthemum tea. "Just like old times."

ॐ

Recadat enters her suite to find it submerged in gloaming, close to pitch-black. She doesn't bother trying to access the room's controls, knowing she would be prevented in any case. The layout is familiar enough, by now, that she is in no danger. In the dark she takes off her jacket, folds it, hangs it on the back of a chair. For a time she sits and closes her eyes, counting her breaths. Any unpredictable event can be met as long as she knows the rhythms of her body; any setback or obstacle can be borne as long as she is anchored by her goals. She thinks of Ayothaya's riverbanks, their endless flowing wealth. On her world rivers are goddesses and the soil itself deific. Every root and fruit and rice grain bears a fragment of the divine.

A hand alights on her jaw. "And how did it go with your mentor, my jewel?"

She tenses. Then relaxes. Her lover's touch always has this effect, an electric current—a shock to the nerves before she remembers what else it entails, the rest of what it can bring. "As smoothly as can be expected. I didn't think she would be here. They made the Court of Divide too attractive. Too much carrot, not enough stick."

A susurrus like scales against velvet. Her lover is sheathed in serpentine accoutrements, in leather that bends as supple as though it is attached to a live animal. "How much did you tell her?"

"You know how much. And how much I didn't tell." The careful balance. Recadat did not tell a single lie, not exactly. Thannarat was once her world, more than Ayothaya itself, more than anyone or anything else. The intensity of passion she felt back then, the lingering regrets after her partner quit the force and disappeared into the fringes of law. Never quite criminal but on the switchblade's edge, a margin so thin there was barely any difference.

"But you didn't tell her about me." Their voice is low and amused, not honey but something that moves slower, sweeter and more fatal. Sugar of lead. "Why not? Don't you trust her?"

"Been ages since we worked together. She must've changed plenty."

Her lover smiles. Their blunt fingernails, painted in jellyfish luminescence, graze along Recadat's throat. They're the only source of illumination in this room and their movement casts odd shadows across her face. They are an antumbral vision. "Yet you feel the same about her, don't you?"

"No." Recadat shivers as a thumb runs across her mouth. Lust lances through her, rousing her fast in the way of drugs. It makes her feel like a lab rat at the mercy of her lover, whose touch summons at will pain or pleasure or a concoction that mingles both. Now the searing lick of a firebrand, now the sudden strike of lightning. Her nipples have pebbled to little points, dark ink against the white of her shirt.

"Don't lie to me, Recadat. I dislike that—your truth belongs to me, and she's the only one from Ayothaya you ever deign to mention." Their fingers circle her throat like a choker, a collar. "Detective Thannarat was your ideal, the plinth on which you rested your beating heart. You told me how masterful you found her, how handsome, how . . . exciting."

"That was before." But her voice is short. The count of her breaths has gone astray.

"Was it, my jewel?" The hand lets go. "Stand up."

She does. Disobedience is not an option. In so short a time they've trained her well, and she both wants and fears what they have to give. Her lover steers her to a full-length mirror. One of the lights snaps to life, the fluorescent cut of it like a whip. She blinks rapidly, disoriented. Her lover has undone her belt, taking off her holster and her gun, knowing that the lack of sidearm makes her feel naked.

"Detective Thannarat," they say against her earlobe. "Do you wish to have what she has, or do you wish to have her?"

"I wish for no such thing. And she was monogamously married when we worked together so there was never a possibility. We have—" Her breath stutters. "We've work to do. An occupying army to repel. Fights to win. She'll cooperate, she has no reason not to."

"Your innocence carries its own appeal, Recadat. What an unblemished gem that is." Her trousers have been slid off. They stroke her inner thigh, hooking into the dip between that and her cunt. She watches their fingers: if she shuts her eyes, they'd make her open them. "You believe in such simple things, hold on to such noble goals. Why not fantasize? When you've got what you want and arrive home the hero of Ayothaya, what shall you ask for? Your world will owe you everything; you can demand it all."

"I'm not demanding anything. The point is to have Ayothaya safe, that's what I . . . "

Their thumb rubs. Their fingers delve. She arches against them, nearly on tiptoes, helplessly watching her own reaction in the mirror: her flushed cheeks, her trembling thighs, her hands scrabbling for purchase. One on the glass, the other on her lover. They are steady the way marble columns are. She clenches her teeth as one finger disappears into her—the wet noise so loud and shameful—and a second follows.

"I like that you're inexperienced." They bite her earlobe, not gently. Pain sings through her like an aphrodisiac freshly imbibed. "You came to me nearly a virgin, and what a delight it has been to teach you about your own responses. All taut strings, all mine to pluck, the gorgeous instrument of you."

Her toes curl. The muscles in her thighs tense. Her mind races ahead, to the point post-climax where she's limp and can barely stay upright, convulsing and clenching down on her lover's fingers. She's not yet there. She soon will be. Her lover knows her nerves and weaknesses so deeply, has mastered every nuance. The exactness of a surgeon.

"With all the pleasure I've shown you, you'd still return to your world an ascetic. So tragic. Don't you want to experiment with what life can truly offer?" A knee nudges her thighs open further. One hand has snaked into her shirt, taking hold of a nipple, twisting it. "Don't you want to do something about Detective Thannarat? Settle your feelings once and for all. Be free."

Free. She's never been that. The map of her life is constrained by obligations, even the matter of Thannarat, the matter that she had to let go or risk her career. Recadat's hands close into fists and finally she shuts her eyes as she imagines that instead of her lover it is Thannarat's fingers in her, Thannarat's voice at her ear. On and on, relentless, a tide that sweeps through and shatters her without end. She'll be as glass, broken to fragments and the fragments broken once more until all that remains is scintillating dust in Thannarat's hand.

எ

The sky is lavender tinged in yellow, a peculiarity of the atmosphere, though the air is clean, more than breathable: nearly untouched by industry of any sort. Enormous ribcages loom, not far, just outside Libretto. No one has been able to find out whether Septet was once ruled by megafauna or whether the machines have terraformed an otherwise unremarkable, uninhabitable planet and filled it with a skeletal bestiary that never was. I'm predisposed to the latter thought. On Shenzhen Sphere, the seat of the Mandate, there are artificial ruins—places that are and have always been red rust and blackened bones, created because one AI or another enjoys desolation as an aesthetic. And nowhere else in the universe does that aesthetic hold truer than on Septet.

Libretto's outskirts overlook an exhausted energy well, where the earth has been carved so deep that this part of the city is a cliff, stark and jagged and stained so many shades by the reinforcements and harvest operations that it is luminescent, falsely beautiful. A chasm of oil-slick radiance and murmuring engine wrecks.

My overlays report elevated radiation and toxin levels. Most people don't live so near the border. Even on this planet, an artificial environment made to support the Mandate's sport, inequality still exists. Perhaps that shouldn't be surprising—Shenzhen is said to be a paradise from the outside, but from the inside it is rumored to be less than perfect.

The residential blocks here are ramshackle, tall narrow buildings bent by time and corrosive elements. Uneven layers of bitumen coat the roofs. Doors are latched shut by bolts or the rare biometric lock, but by and large anyone can pass through. I don't call ahead: the person I want doesn't have the implants necessary for overlays. Has had them excised long ago, unless something's changed.

Stepping into this building exposes an unpleasant truth. The Vimana is lavish, contemporary and sanitized. The floor of this place has borne witness to accrued strata of filth, dried blood and effluvia from plumbing failures. Its walls are pockmarked by wear and tear, by sudden violence.

I knock on a door that is better reinforced than most. It opens just a fraction; I'm let in and the door shuts immediately, as though to prevent the conditioned air inside from escaping. The room's sole resident double-locks the door, bolting then securing it with a matrix that looks several generations out of date.

"Detective." He attempts a stiff smile. "It's been a minute."

"You look well," I say, though he doesn't.

He's thinner than I remember, loose-skinned, a wattle trembling beneath his chin. Pale to the point of gray, cheeks receded to the outline of his skull. His nose juts oddly as though it belongs to a much more dignified, patrician face. Bulging eyes that always seem afflicted by fundamental tragedy, hair the color of acid-blanched bricks. When he seats himself he does so gingerly, as though he thinks any moment the furniture might turn against him and swallow him whole. His name is Ostrich, the English word for a type of flightless bird—I've looked it up; strange-looking creature. When I first heard it, I thought his name sounded vaguely Germanic. In truth he came from the Catania Protectorate, so the name his parents or government gave him was likelier to be Italian. Giovanni or Giovanna or such; I'm not familiar either way.

"I've been worse." Ostrich crosses his legs, uncrosses them, rearranges them and settles with them akimbo. "Didn't expect to see you here. Didn't expect visitors. Septet—terrible place. How's your wife?"

"We divorced." I don't add that Eurydice is dead. Has been for eight years.

"Oh." He inclines his head awkwardly. "My condolences. Eurydice was a lovely lady."

She was more than that; she was resplendent and she was the world. But I'm not here to wax nostalgic about my ex-wife with him when he barely knew her. I hold up a card I've loaded with a tidy sum. More than he earns here in a month, by my estimate. "Tell me everything you know about the Court of Divide."

"You really don't do pleasantries."

"I do them perfectly well with attractive women." I give him a half-shrug. "I can ask after your health, if you like."

He eyes the card. Estimating and speculating how much is in there. The disadvantage of having no overlays. "You wouldn't care anyway. Are you here for the—because of what happened to Ayothaya?"

"I have a feeling," I say blandly, "that *what happened* will be the only thing people know about Ayothaya for several generations."

Those first bombardments, that first monstrous contact when the Hellenic army fell down upon us like ravening beasts. The Javelin of Hellenes is a polity that fancies themselves a nation of warriors and has been known to strike almost randomly, without cause or warning. Still, they pretended at honor, at heeding humane rules of engagement: no targeting of civil centers, medical institutions, aid stations. Who can complain? Plenty of armies would have done much worse. We could have been sacked by the Armada of Amaryllis.

The entire event—I can think of it with distance, now.

I angle the card this way and that, watching it glint, watching it catch Ostrich's eye. "The invasion is someone else's business—I'm here for a different reason, and I'm a little offended you would assume. My interest in Septet could be academic. Just because I look like a brute doesn't mean I cannot pursue intellectual passions."

Ostrich knows better than to scoff. Instead he moves stiffly to a filing cabinet. Even before the invasion, he was an unusual man: partial to antique means of recording, pen and paper, ink and lamination; even a few nielloware plates that he etched himself. Despite the distance he's put between his present and former lives, he keeps mementos of his heritage and faith. Crucifixes of various sizes stand in his room, some empty and others burdened by the bleeding messiah. Statuettes of the virgin mother (now possible with womb-tanks; likely impossible during the prehistory of his religious apocrypha) either carrying her dead son or draped in garlands.

I lean against the wall, steering clear of the delicate statuettes. Wherever I go, I intrude upon fragile things. Lovers have ever told me I'm a creature of rough edges, rough strength, like an avalanche.

He produces a folder—an actual folder, plastic and aluminum, holding within it a wealth of papers. "Here."

Ostrich's pastime is sociology, and when I learned where he disappeared to, I understood his reason immediately—not just that Septet is out of the way and digitally isolated, but because it is a unique world. Constructed entirely to host the Court of Divide, yet not to function as an integrated state like Shenzhen. Instead it is more of a colony, and not a favored one.

Many of his notes are on the sociopolitical impact on the population, on how even the most basic elements of the tournament affect everyday life, transforming Septet into an economy of savage needs and carnivorous prices. There is rarely a lull between rounds—

as soon as a victor is declared and infrastructure has been repaired, the next one begins immediately. Human residents amount to less than ten million, which makes this world essentially deserted. Most were selected from migrants aspiring to enter Shenzhen; they have been promised life in the Dyson sphere once they've served their time here. Septet as a halfway house with every inmate held to strict demands of conduct: perform as props for the Court of Divide and eventually earn admission to utopia.

Out of this population, some have themselves entered the game; plenty have ignobly perished. It is an exploitative equation, not that the Mandate requires Septet residents to participate. But consent given in desperation—to be out of here and in Shenzhen Sphere—is hardly true agency.

All this I already know. What I'm after is his case notes. Fortunately I learned his handwriting while he was on Ayothaya; his scribbling is difficult enough that it comprises encryption all its own. I flip through and find records of precedents where regalia killed their own duelists or where duelists destroyed their own regalia. The kind of information off-world Divide aficionados could not have found out, since what transpires on the ground is so secretive.

I scan the pages, collating them and setting the file aside in my overlays, then hand the folder back to Ostrich. "You must make a decent living selling this to new duelists."

"I get by."

"Is Septet," I go on, "truly the Mandate's only territory outside Shenzhen?"

His head jerks as though he's been stung or slapped. "I can't answer that, Detective. I don't even know. Do you think the AIs come over here and tell me all their political decisions? Give me a roadmap of where they'll set up shop next?"

Fair enough. "Did you ever see any of these people?" I present to him the reconstructed images. "Plus a woman from One Thousand Erhus—aristocratic, likely, well-bred and used to comfort? And an enforcer from the Vatican?"

"I've met them." He names all but one as well as their regalia. The entire time he eyes the crucifixes nervously as though he hopes they could fold into an armored fort around him, a Catholic protection from the capricious universe.

"One last question. I'm given to understand that a regalia is limited to a single proxy and once it's destroyed, that's that for the AI and they're out of the game. Is this a hard-and-fast rule?"

Ostrich's exhalation is ragged, adrenaline and remembered pain. I'm not the first to have asked him dangerous questions. "Not always," he says at length. "There are game rules and then there are Mandate laws. One flexes, the other doesn't. You better stay on your toes, Detective."

Once, on a frigid morning, I found him outside the walls of the Catanian consulate, bloody and weeping. He'd slit his own wrist. It was an inefficient method and the location public; he'd meant to be found. I gave him first aid and accompanied him to a clinic. Later I dragged him to a nearby bar—the kind that opens round the clock— and bought him mocktails until he stopped crying. He never did tell me why he'd attempted suicide, and soon after he disappeared entirely. It took time to track him to Septet. A world for lost things.

"Always." I hand him the card. "Thanks, Ostrich. I'll come back if I need anything else."

CHAPTER TWO

Good sense would direct me back to the Vimana, but the truth is that the hotel offers no more safety than anywhere else: outside the Cenotaph, all refuge is illusory. I instead choose to wander a while near the residential block, noting as I do how few people there are, how unnatural the demographic distribution is. Since I've arrived, I have seen few children and no elderly, nor have I observed any apparent family. Those who have volunteered to live here must be primarily unattached or have forsaken their previous lives, or they're criminals removed from their original societies. It makes me think of militaries. The last chance at redemption or upward mobility, the naked exploitation of those with nothing left to lose.

I circle back to the faded energy well, where a sight catches my eye. A petite figure stands at the cliff's edge, poised with one foot forward hovering on empty air. You can never tell what seeing this chasm does to someone, the luminescent cliff, the undulating light. We're attracted to the plummet, and this person's weight is balanced on the single foot still on the cliff, shod in a shoe whose heel tapers to a needlepoint. I walk faster.

Their face, in profile, is perfect in the way of extensive modifications or mannequin integument. Luminous, poreless skin. They lean forward.

I'm mid-sprint when they leap.

A flash of brilliance. I reach the precipice in time to see the person change, mid-plunge. Not a person—an AI; a regalia. Wings unfurl from its back, enormous, like feathered pyres. Rationally I know those are antigravity kites, but the spectacle of it catches me by surprise all the same. The regalia's corona outshines the energy well's remnants: gold and pearl, a hundred sunrises condensed. Blinding, literally so.

My optical filters adjust. When my vision clears, I see a second figure rising out of the chasm, meeting the winged regalia blow for blow. They're fast. I've seen combat of all kinds, the meticulous and the spontaneous, between trained soldiers and between criminals tutored by the streets. None of it was like this. The regalia fight with weapons too large for any human to wield, glaive against spear, the blades of them flowing and reflowing as they make contact. The second AI is a creature made featureless by their armor—a sheath of fluid black, oil-sheened, that absorbs each strike it receives and instantly reforms. A complex type of ablative protection, visually obfuscated by its own rapid phase-shifts.

Abruptly I realize I'm in too open a space. This is not an entertainment put on for me to safely watch. My sensors detect no immediate threats, but I don't have access to municipal or satellite surveillance the way I did on Ayothaya. Ostrich's block isn't far and I am nearly there when my overlays flash a warning vector.

I dive under the ramshackle roof of an old storage. Exposed architecture cracks and dissolves: I determine immediately that the ammunition is large-bore, and that the shot was made by a human. An AI would not have missed and, more importantly, would have struck with something much deadlier and harder to avoid than a conventional bullet.

Calculations wheel in the corner of my vision as I run through the warehouse—the duelist is a sharpshooter. The vector originated from two and a half kilometers away: decent, nothing remarkable, and they do not have access to anything in the orbit that would have conferred greater range and precision.

My imaging and the navigation Wonsul's Exegesis provided let me know that I'm near a mausoleum, one of the larger buildings in this area and which—importantly—has a basement. I review the footage I captured of the fighting regalia, but it is less informative than I'd prefer. At least it doesn't look like either of them is deploying transatmospheric artillery. That should keep me safe for some time.

I run up against a corrugated door. There is no time for subtlety. I step back and slam my fist into the lock. It gives in a crumbling of brittle mortar and oxidized metal.

The space behind it is wide, high-ceilinged, the floor tiled in mosaic the color of antique gold and worn jade. A patina of dust clings to everything as though nobody's been in here for a long time—possible: this is not a Divide facility, not a place of commerce or accommodation. I wend deeper, looking for the staircase that'd bring me to the basement and from there to the maintenance warren beneath Libretto.

I pass rows of sarcophagi: some are stone, others milky glass or blackened steel, and none have been disturbed. One exception—a bronze casket with its lid agape, the contents within on full display. Despite my need for haste, I slow down. The corpse is perfectly preserved, pale in the way of new ivory rather than the gray of dead flesh, and drowned in fox pelts: a wealth of blazing electrum and copper, immaculate and untarnished. The body's mouth is filled with roses so fresh they're radiant with dew, petals dawn-pink and bruise-red, such a surfeit of them that they spill out. Down the chin, scattered along the throat and collarbones. Whoever it is was buried nude.

A roar like muted thunder. The mausoleum's wall falls apart in a shower of smashed stone and riven reinforcement. Behind it is the regalia with the gold wings and the glaive, their expression as serene as a bodhisattva's.

I've faced death before: I've learned to keep moving, to not freeze up, as I clasp eyes with what might be the last thing I ever see. I have kept one step, two steps, ahead of my mortality. To do otherwise is to die like a dumb beast.

But at this moment there's nothing I can do, no action I can take to avert what is about to fall. No bullet is fast enough, and fleeing is futile.

My overlays light up and roses suffuse my vision. A voice whispers in my ear, *You only get one chance to answer, duelist. Do you belong to me?*

"Yes," I say, on sheer instinct.

A flood of song: for a moment I can't tell whether it is virtual or exists as a physical fact, the percussion that vibrates through my bones, the high ringing notes that fill my skull. A new module registers in my overlays, bannering a short message. *Duelist acknowledged. Welcome to the Court of Divide. To victory eternal.*

The golden regalia strikes. Its glaive is caught by a crimson sword, broad, the edge of it faint blue-black. I observe every detail—the intricacy of each regalia's weapon: how well made both are, how thoughtfully fashioned, the etched motifs. In such moments the world is written out with stunning clarity.

What I thought a picturesque corpse stands tall before me, a splendor of petaled pelts and precious metals. Now animated and acutely alive, long-backed and wide-hipped: beautiful in the way of water's mirage in the desert.

It—she—glances over her shoulder, meeting my gaze. Then she turns to the other regalia and says, "It's indecorous to pick on an unarmed human, don't you think?"

The other regalia doesn't answer. It adjusts its glaive, folding its wings into its back. Its next blow carves the mosaic open and splits the tiles. The rose regalia—mine—guards against it almost without effort, holding her weapon one-handed. She pushes the enemy back, and back again, driving it out of the mausoleum. Dust rises in spumes.

On my feet, I keep to the cover the shattered wall provides; what little visibility I have I use to scan for the next attack from the duelist who shot at me. Nothing yet. I draw my gun, clasping the cold weight of it and contemplating the ammunition with which it is loaded. An AI proxy built for combat—and all of them would be, on Septet—is a potent weapon, obliteration incarnate. Not invulnerable, however; nothing is. Weapon labs across the galaxies have dedicated themselves to designing anti-proxy armaments. Of course they're as destructible as anything else, but most people can't carry around artillery of the appropriate caliber. An AI usually keeps its core somewhere safe while its physical representation is deployed on the field. What gunsmiths focus on, obsess over, is how to snip the link between proxy and AI.

The two regalia are more like phantasms than reality, palinopsia of gold on red, too fast for me to track. But optical assists allow me to distinguish between them, enough to sight down and fire. The range isn't so terrible.

Show me some trust, duelist. The same voice as before, sonorous, operatic. A music of lily and bergamot. *What good am I as a regalia if I can't fend off a little thing like this?*

From my perspective the golden regalia is hardly little. Petite-figured, but so is the rose regalia, who moves like a fox's poem. I lower my gun. It is not a good time in any case. This is too early to show two AIs that I possess anti-machine weaponry.

The decisive strike comes abruptly: a flash of red, fired seemingly from nowhere, that arrows through the golden regalia. It lands. A fox, long-toothed, with a proxy leg clenched between its jaw.

The gilded creature teeters. It rights itself, balancing precariously on one foot, wings extending. In a heartbeat it is off the ground, the match abandoned.

My regalia strides over to me. Even outside of combat she moves with peculiar grace, as if her feet are not quite touching the ground—as if she is walking on a bed of roses, an orchard she owns and whose produce she is exclusively entitled to. The petals and pelts shift around her, mantling and draping her limbs, not quite baring her to the elements but close: little is left to the imagination. The fox, her second proxy, trots after her.

"I am Empress Daji Scatters Roses Before Her Throne. Call me Daji." She holds out a wrist corsaged in roses—some as tiny as pearls, others nearly as large as her hand. "The regalia to your duelist."

I take her hand and bring my mouth to a spot of pseudoskin: surprisingly soft, in fine mimesis of the organic counterpart. My lips brush over the petals, unavoidably. Delicate. They must be part of her, joined to the proxy's sensory subsystem. "And I'm the duelist to your regalia. My name you must already know."

Daji's mouth—gold too, with subtle flecks of green—curves, and her knuckle touches my cheek. "Thus our contract is sealed: with a kiss. I enjoy chivalry, Khun Thannarat, and while I select my partners for their aesthetic appeal it's not every round I find someone as suited to my tastes as you."

I let go. "My impression is that machines don't care for human values of attraction."

"Many don't," she agrees. "I do. Or rather, what humans consider beautiful happens to match my definition of beauty and you, my wielder, are delicious to look at. Your manners are fantastic too, always a plus. Shall we retire to somewhere more comfortable?"

From raging battle to this. Such whiplash. I eye the little fox that has climbed to her shoulders, curling about her like a scarf. "I have a room at the Vimana."

"Ah, a woman of taste *and* means." Her raiment of fur and flowers meld, reshaping into something more closely resembling clothing. "There, I should look human enough."

"And your second proxy?" I don't ask why she's been able to circumvent that particular rule.

"It's not a real, full proxy." Daji grins and it is a hungry slash; her teeth are too sharp and too long. "This is more of an accessory. Believable even for an ordinary person, isn't it? Come. If you run into anyone you know, you may introduce me as an untamed fox you found in the wild."

৵

Daji makes herself at home in my suite. The first thing she does is reconfigure her clothing again to something less modest, a sheath so diminutive it hardly deserves the appellation, backless and strapless. Her creamy breasts are covered by a mesh of claret strands but only just. A gold choker encircles her throat. I visualize tugging on it, twisting it, finding the point of her pulse. But there would be no pulse, unless she simulates it.

She unfolds the suite's bar and plucks out two long-stemmed glasses. "The selection here is as decent as you can get on a world so remote. What do you like, Detective? Vodka, wine, whiskey? Sake, perhaps?"

"Pick for me. I'm interested in your preferences. The choice of liquor can tell you a lot about a person." Though she's not a person in the sense that I am a person. Regardless we're long past the point of whether AIs have souls—the answer has been moot the moment they broke away from us and created their own society. Souls cannot be touched, counted, measured. Military and political might can.

Her laugh is airy. The movement of her thighs is anything but. Her skirt parts and closes and winds around her long legs, animated fabric

33

that whispers against her skin as though offering a taste of what is to come. "My pick, then." She fills both glasses: vodka of considerable strength, pooling pure and clear. "So then, what's a woman like you doing on a world like this? Your great wish. That which brought you here in madness, to risk life and limb and eternity."

I've met machines before; none are as human as she—Wonsul's Exegesis looks obviously alien compared to this. I could almost believe she is mortal, albeit more silicon and tubing than tissue and endothelium. A woman whose innards burn like little stars, whose limbs are guided by actuators and engine precision, liberated from the foibles of the flesh. "You aren't like any AI I've ever seen."

"That is because you have never seen us masquerading as humans before, or if you have you didn't notice." Daji sips from her glass. "I'll tell you that, initially, it was the eating and drinking that gave us trouble. Organic digestion is severely inefficient and what we did was to incinerate any food that passed our mouths, which meant we had to dedicate a little chamber to the task, and a proxy's insides are precious real estate . . . Say, you're very curious about whether we've expanded our territory beyond Shenzhen and Septet, aren't you? What a wild universe it would be if we could turn up anywhere, wreaking havoc and working mischief. Half the time you wouldn't even realize it's us. How terrifying it must be for you."

For the moment she's letting me steer the conversation away from the subject of my goals. "You've been surveilling me," I say. "Since when?"

"Matchmaking algorithms require an enormity of data, Detective, and our contract goes deeper than any marriage. Why shouldn't I learn about potential duelists as much as possible? Until you came along, nobody caught my eye—I thought I was going to sit this one out. They're all very banal. They are obsessed with rules. *You* didn't even care that we weren't taking new aspirants at this juncture."

I drink. The vodka goes down like cold fire. "Only because I have an advantage."

"Benzaiten is the thorn in the side of all upstanding machines." Daji uncoils her fox proxy and sets it on the ground; it pads over to the corner and curls up. "Luckily I'm upstanding in no way. I assume that even though you acted in contravention of the Divide's laws, you're familiar with them. The first clause in the duelist-regalia pact is that I will not reveal any information to you that may injure or expose the Mandate. The second clause is that I will not reveal any information that's privy to the Divide system, meaning that I'm not disclosing the names of other regalia or duelists, nor certain corollaries and secrets."

"Very fair." I draw up the Divide module and project it on the wall. The data it yields is scant—just the number of duelists and regalia still active, and a count of aspirants. Aspirants: one. Regalia: five. Duelists: eighteen. "This is *much* fewer than I expected."

"One of the pairs has been on a killing spree." Daji puts her index finger to her lips. "The duelist of that pair you'll need to discover for yourself. The regalia is the one I fought on your behalf."

"How potent are you in combat, compared to the rest of the surviving regalia?"

"My, I could take that question as an insult." She holds up her hand, examining her fingernails. "Five times I've participated in the Court of Divide. Two times I've guided my duelist to victory; two times I've guided them to survival, sparing them the loser's fate. As regalia go, I'm a true prize, Detective."

I look at her, taking in the entirety of her. Machines may lie. She could be boasting and I will never be able to verify it. "My understanding," I say, "is that as the game progresses, duelists may compete in ceremonies that grant them or their regalia access to Septet's offensive systems. Armaments, orbital scans, long-range artillery."

"And you think I've missed out on those, putting me at a disadvantage. I plan to surprise you." The AI steps close, taking the empty glass from my hand. She turns the rim of it along the line of my throat. "I plan to surprise you a lot. Oh, and you did make contact with a defeated duelist, didn't you? Wring her dry for information—I recommend it. As long as you don't seduce her all the way into this room."

An oddly chiding tone. "Because you value privacy?"

"Oh, Detective, you can be so coy. Will you want to shower and rest? It must've been a long day for you."

I could say that I'm not tired, but the truth is that I'm far from fresh and in any case Daji is already sliding off my overcoat: she's made the decision for me. The way she removes my coat is deliberate, as though she's unpeeling a gift she's long anticipated. Up close, the difference in height between us is even starker. I'm a hundred eighty-nine centimeters and her proxy is barely one sixty, perhaps to have a small profile in battle. But at a glance she looks delicate, and her pale fingers—gliding over the armored panels of my shirt—belong on a pianist or harpist.

"I can undress myself." My voice is a little thick. Ridiculous. She is an AI.

Her hand pauses on the buckle of my belt, thumb hooked into the waistband of my trousers. "You're sure you don't want me to join you in the bath? I imagine there are things in your luggage and wardrobe you don't want me to poke at."

"You can peruse whatever you like." Not a single spot on Septet is hidden from the Mandate: the contents of my luggage have already been scanned and recorded by the Vimana's surveillance and therefore visible to Wonsul's Exegesis. Whether Daji finds my specialized ammunition offensive I will discover in time.

By habit I shower thoroughly and quickly, the product of a profession where I was often roused out of bed in the middle of the night to attend urgent cases. Once I'm clean, I put on a touch of cologne. Mildly absurd before bed, but I am vain in my own ways.

I return to the bedroom in boxer briefs and a Vimana robe—deep brown with hints of garnet, the fabric silken—to find Daji has taken up the bed, reclining half-covered in the sheets. What I can see of her is bare entirely. No more diminutive sheath, though the choker remains.

"Should I gallantly offer to sleep on the couch?"

She raises her head from where it is propped on the pillow. "Certainly not, you know I don't need to rest. I've been keeping this warm for you. Climb on in, Detective. I'm excellent at providing comfort in bed, you can think of me as a sleep therapy device."

I stay where I am, crossing my arms. "Why this?"

Her head cranes from side to side; I'm treated to the spectacle of the cords in her throat in motion, the way they draw the eye to the siren song of her neck. Where it descends to join the shoulders, where the collarbones bloom like fruits that must be tasted, licked, bitten. "For the duration of this contest, Detective, I want you to belong to me entirely or to no one at all. And when I say entirely, I mean that. In all possible ways."

My pulse rises. My imagination sparks; I tamp that down—here more than ever I cannot let my libido do the thinking. "Machines don't congress with humans." There are rumors, naturally there would be.

"A handful does. Am I not comely in your eyes?" She tosses her head; again that tactical accentuation of her throat—here is her invitation, come get it if you dare.

I do not, as yet, dare. "We've only just met. And I do need the sleep."

Her gilded mouth pulls into a moue. "I shall be patient. I may remain in bed?"

First the demand then the concession, the push then the pull. It is alluring, calculated to be so. "Of course. This isn't sanctuary ground; how else would you guard me?"

I dim the light further as I get in until it is near-dark. Truth be told, it's been so long since I spent the night with anyone. My trysts since my divorce have been numerous: women are doors and I am a key that turns many locks. But I would send them away once the deed—and aftercare, if any is needed—is done. Having another body in bed as I settle in for rest is different, vulnerable.

Then again, what lies next to me can slaughter dozens of humans without trying. Asleep or awake, I'm vulnerable to her just the same.

Her arm snakes around me from behind as she tucks herself against me, and even through the fabric, I can feel that externally she has emulated human epidermis without flaw. Soft breasts against my spine, soft hand against my belly. I wonder at her anatomy and immediately quash that idea.

"Oakmoss and ambergris," she murmurs against my shoulder. "Such a fine, rich choice. Is this your sole cologne?"

"Typically I carry one. Yes."

"There's a perfumer in this building. They make a mix that will suit you excellently—saffron, oud, and heart of violet; quite striking. Plus another one that is mostly vetiver . . . you must let me buy you a sampler or three."

"Are you this attentive to all your duelists?"

"All? No, only one and even then she was not a duelist. A favored human, that's all."

"What happened to her?"

"She became lost." Daji's hand withdraws. "Go to sleep, Detective. By your circadian data you need six hours to be fully rested, and I want you to be at your best."

I wake up to a call tinkling gently in my overlays. Six in the morning, beginning of dawn. The curtains part a sliver at my command and Septet's sun peers in, dappling the bed and the soft floor in ovals and oblongs. My regalia remains at my side, to all appearances asleep. The fox proxy though is active and follows me to the bathroom to watch me clean my mouth and rinse my face. I let Recadat know we'll meet in my private lounge, a perk for Vimana guests who pay for sufficiently expensive suites.

Daji's lesser body has made itself small enough to climb into my robe and nestle in one of its inner pockets. I look at the bed askance, but the primary proxy remains stubbornly unresponsive, chest rising and falling to simulate deep sleep. "Not a morning person," I say aloud and stroke down the fox's head, its spine, its feast of textural extravagance. More luxurious than silk or velour, similar to how nacre might feel if it's spun into a pelt.

The temperature in the lounge is warmer than I'd like, subject to an algorithmic whim of the Vimana. I shrug the robe partially off, make myself comfortable on one of the large chairs, and wait for the air to cool.

Recadat is punctual. She stops short when she sees my state of undress. "Can't you put on some clothes?"

"I'm clothed. You've seen me actually naked before." Was there, in fact, when I lost both my legs. She was the one who gave me covering fire and dragged me to the medics. An entire quarter of the city was a warzone that night from a syndicate dispute gone out of control.

"Different context. I can't believe you went and got yourself even *more* scars."

I pass my hand over my chest, where a rope of pale tissue crosses between my breasts. "I enjoy having them—think of them as combat medals." The only ones I've had corrected and removed were those that interfered with nerve or muscle function. Recadat has a different view; she has had all of hers erased.

My old partner snorts as she drops into a chaise lounge. "Sometimes you talk like an ex-soldier, not an ex-cop."

"There isn't a lot of difference between the military and public safety." Both being state-sanctioned agents of ruin, frequently indiscriminate and occasionally interchangeable. Institutions of violence differ only in budget and uniforms.

Recadat makes a noise that tells me she knows exactly what I mean, and that she vehemently disagrees with my perspective. Her belief is that public security keeps the peace whereas the army breaks it. "What's been happening in your life, anyway? I know you got a divorce but not much else."

That must've slipped onto the grapevine somehow, even though I cut contact with former colleagues after handing in my resignation and disabling my badge. "Eurydice is gone."

She startles. "During the invasion?"

"No, she left Ayothaya long before the Hellenes happened. Maybe she knew something we didn't." But I say this dryly, not particularly meaning it. Eurydice was not saved where she went.

"I'm sorry." Recadat twists her small hands in her lap. She's never been good at informing next-of-kin that their spouse or relation has been reduced to a casualty statistic—too much empathy. On my part I've always made it quick: the boil needs to be lanced, as it were, and no one—other than Recadat—goes into public security to become grief counselors. "I know you loved her completely. Thoroughly."

"Not enough," I say. "Not as much as she deserved. I was never any good at marriage." Had coasted, before that, on the ease of temporary trysts. The flash burn of passion, not the steadiness of matrimony.

Recadat looks like she wants to say something, but she refrains. For no logical reason I watch her delicate fingers and think of Eurydice's, even though these two have nothing in common. My ex-wife was nearly as tall as I am whereas Recadat is petite, a hundred fifty-five. Not fragile: she's sinewy and economic. Eurydice was more like a rose apple, ripe and luscious. My tastes range widely, but I try not to think of Recadat in those terms anymore. Especially now, when I cannot afford the distraction.

"So." She shifts in her seat, crossing her legs. "Did you get a regalia?"

"Yes." I don't ask how she guessed; both of us read people for a living. "Do you hold duelist overrides?"

"Well, don't you get things done fast. A whole regalia one day after landing." She quirks an eyebrow. "Allow me to make a little guess. Your AI looks like a pretty woman. Slinky legs, tiny dress, hair down to their haunch. You have a type."

"I have more than one type." I never strayed from the bounds of marriage, but Recadat witnessed me appreciating women of a particular style and bearing often enough. Even if she did not quite notice me appreciating *her* in that manner, or was kind enough to pretend obliviousness because she did not return it. "And AIs can look however they want, Recadat. The overrides?"

"I've got three—I can give you two; I'm keeping one just in case, maybe I'll even need it to rescue you in a pinch."

"Works for me." The fox inside my robe nibbles at my hip, not breaking skin but clearly irate. "We discussed the other duelists in passing; care to tell me a bit more? I want to work with a full deck."

"Before that . . . " She hesitates. "You do know what happens if you're one of the final two duelists standing and you lose?"

Out of habit I needlessly smooth down my hair. I keep it chin-length, artificially treated so as to need minimal care. "Yes, the loser submits their mortal coil to machine uses. Experiments, I assume, most likely unpleasant. Maybe execution or torture as a spectacle— some machines must be into that."

She grimaces. "You say it so casually. But you play to win, so it's not going to happen to you anyway. I'm sending you the intel I've gathered. Faces, names, habits, vices. The usual."

Recadat's data package blooms in my overlays, gravid with footage and stills. I draw up my leg and prop my ankle on my knee. "I've been rude. I haven't asked at all what you've been up to."

"After you quit, I got transferred a couple times then transferred back. They promoted me to captain of our subdivision, lined me up to be commander in a few years. Then the invasion happened and all of that stopped meaning anything."

"It'll start meaning something again. The pay raise must've been something to celebrate, at least. Did you ever settle down? Ten years are a long while." No point asking about her biological family—like me, she doesn't keep in touch. We're similar in that way, detached from kin and rootless. By choice for me—I don't care for most of my family, and my parents divorced long before I reached my majority—and less so for her. A transport malfunction orphaned Recadat when she was twelve, and as far as I know the aunt that raised her treated her as a bitter ordeal. Not so much malicious abuse as indifferent neglect, providing her no more than the bare minimum.

Recadat gives an embarrassed little laugh. "You remember that I wanted to start a family. Gave up on it, though. I never did get the one woman I wanted."

"No? But you were so popular. Half the rookies were in love with you. There was that Internal Affairs woman, remember, she was so besotted she let you go without a single bit of paperwork."

She waves her hand. "Sure. They weren't what I wanted, though. It's as if—you want chicken tendon fried just so, all spicy and sour. But you keep getting served sweet potato balls. Bowls of coconut cream and egg floss. Platters of meringue. I wanted to chew something tough and savory, not dry-swallow sugary air. As for popular, *you* caught more eyes than I ever did. You never felt tempted?"

From anyone else I'd find the question offensive; from her it is merely natural. We had a push-pull relationship, blunt and inquisitive in some matters and closed off in others. "I'm particular. One woman at a time." A lie: Recadat tempted me. As close as I ever got to risking my marriage. Ironic that something else entirely led to my divorce.

"You can be such a monk," she murmurs, which is rich coming from someone who lived in near-celibacy. "I wish I'd gotten to know Eurydice better—I got the impression she didn't like law enforcement and only tolerated your job because she was head over heels . . . Well. Enough about the past. So, the other duelists. The one you'll want to keep an eye on is Ouru, family name unknown, origins unknown. Zer regalia is Houyi's Chariot, a proxy masked and armored in blue-black. No idea what it looks like underneath. About your height give or take a couple centimeters, their build a lot like yours. Other duelists might even think you're Houyi in disguise."

Ouru, I would guess, was the one who shot at me near the energy well. "What in particular makes zer stand out?"

Recadat makes a face. "I lost my regalia to zer. But ze's vicious and completely willing to kill."

"I don't imagine anyone here is *not* willing to kill. I saw Houyi's Chariot fighting a small regalia, golden armor, wings. Any idea about that one?"

"Chun Hyang's Glaive," she says. "Extremely destructive, partnered to a woman named Ensine Balaskas. They're the ones who have been slaughtering duelists and aspirants at a fast clip. Might even have caught a few non-participants, actually, though it can be hard to tell."

"Are there hidden benefits to murdering random bystanders?" I contemplate, for a microsecond or so, whether I'd be willing to try if it gives me a leg up in the game.

"Not that I know of. My read of Balaskas is that she's just a common serial murderer."

Spree murderer, but I don't correct her. I'm not here to be a criminology pedant and besides, she's had more official experience. "She killed a man from the Vatican, a woman from One Thousand Erhus, and what I assumed was a coterie of allied duelists."

Recadat shakes her head. "They grouped up to challenge Balaskas. I told them it was a terrible idea. One thing I'll say for Ensine Balaskas is that she's predictable—if she wants someone dead, she sends a calling card to invite them to a match. You could have a field day building her criminal profile."

The kind of killer who fancies herself an artist: the disembowelment and mutilation must have been a part of that conceit. "I look forward to receiving mine. I assume she's the likeliest to come for me first." Given that I eluded her regalia out in the energy wells. "Say— you're staying in the Vimana, aren't you? It could be useful if we're close by. Would you consider relocating to my floor, maybe to an adjacent suite? We should be able to open an interconnection."

Inside my robe, the fox grazes my elbow with its teeth. Extremely sharp, a promise.

For no reason I can discern, Recadat looks down and away. Gaze darting anywhere but me. "I'm only a couple floors below yours. Proximate enough—I'd make a terrible roommate. Have you seen how I deal with my laundry?"

"As you like." The fox settles. My arm is safe for the moment. "Would you mind telling me the name of your fallen regalia?"

She gives me a look. "You want to have the entire picture—you always did. His name was Gwalchmei Bears Lilies. My bad luck to have acquired a regalia so poor, but here we are. Better luck with yours, Thannarat."

Two overrides appear in my Divide module as she leaves. I give them a cursory look, wondering why Recadat turned so short with me. Perhaps Gwalchmei—what a mouthful—is a sore spot.

I turn my attention back to Ostrich's notes. He has recorded previous victors here and there, names unfamiliar to me, like Captain Erisant of the Seven-Sung Fleet and some soldier from Mahakala. I focus on the regalia. Daji appears several times, as does Chun Hyang's Glaive. The comprehensiveness of his files—almost a cheat sheet, encyclopedic—makes me wonder why no duelist has killed him to prevent competitors from obtaining this, but then I realize he must live under the overseer's protection. For one reason or another, his faithful chronicling serves the Mandate's purposes. His accounts corroborate Daji's boasts: that she's fought many times and most of her duelists have won or at least survived.

Seven times Chun Hyang's Glaive has joined the Divide. Seven times it has won.

Improbable. Not that Ostrich has a reason to lie, and yet like any other information I gather on Septet it is challenging to verify. I may pay him another visit, just in case. He has not recorded anything on Houyi's Chariot or Gwalchmei Bears Lilies—this round might be their debuts.

I put the file away and review Recadat's. The folder includes what Ensine Balaskas and Ouru look like. I compare those to what I saw at the tearoom. No match, either in patrons or staff; a shame.

"I don't imagine you could organize these files for me," I say to Daji. "A little indexing assistance."

The fox twitches against me. Coral petals flutter through my overlays. *I only do that for duelists I've gotten very, very close to, Detective. And we're not close, are we? As you said, we've just met. Now that Recadat, you two must have been awfully close. You should ask her to index her files better.*

"Did you practice sulking or are you a natural at it?"

She does not dignify that with an answer; the fox proxy darts out of my robe, disappearing back into the suite.

An announcement unfurls in the Divide module as I'm browsing the Vimana breakfast menu. Wonsul's Exegesis has declared the final sub-contest to obtain an override, to take place in the city of Cadenza. Duelists who wish to compete are prohibited from bringing or receiving direct assistance from their regalia.

I order my food and finish eating quickly. There is a shuttle to Cadenza leaving in a couple hours. Daji remains in bed, her back turned to me, her head artfully arranged. I stop by, run my hand through the dark tributaries of her hair, and kiss her shoulder. "I'll be back soon." If she wants me to treat her like a human woman, I can oblige. Maybe even AIs enjoy roleplaying.

The fox proxy licks my hand, rubbing its velvet face against my palm. All is forgiven, for now.

CHAPTER THREE

The shuttle to Cadenza is more crowded than I would expect, filled with people who look ordinary enough, just commuting. I find my seat and settle in, surveying the other rows. Eighteen duelists remain, seven without regalia and five with. A fair number would be aboard this shuttle; many would know each other's face already, and Ouru would recognize mine through zer regalia.

Ze does a good job of appearing nondescript—a honeyed complexion undecorated by dermals or scars, a face that could belong anywhere, plain well-fitted kurta and pants. Southeast Asian, I'd say, and therefore ze might have come from any number of polities; we have that in common. Tiny earrings, white gold or electrum; no rings or bracelets that would get in the way in combat. Zer hands are spatulate, lightly callused around the thumbs. Ambidextrous.

I lean across my seat. "I'm Thannarat." My name offered as goodwill. "I don't suppose we could talk?"

Ouru doesn't pretend surprise. "More privately, please."

We open a link. I fold my hands and make a show of looking out the window, to a view of Septet's ruinscape. There is not much forestry in this part of the equator, and the land is a vastness of jaundiced earth broken up by those impossible skeletons. A few look reptilian while others look like they could have been chimeras, horned and long-hoofed but with inexplicable primate features.

You're the new duelist. The last one. How did you survive Chun Hyang's Glaive?

The usual way, I inform zer, *by not dying. I trust Houyi's Chariot is well?*

Ze unwraps a protein bar—it smells surprisingly good, savory with shallots and dried meats—and begins to eat. *Houyi is the only remaining regalia who stands a chance of contesting Chun Hyang. That should inform your forthcoming decisions.*

My smile is slow. In my fogged reflection in the window, it looks like a gash. I don't bother demanding redress for zer attempt to snipe me down. *Certainly I'll take it into account. May I ask why you spared the duelist Recadat?*

Ouru's head twitches. *Ah. She's the one who told you about me. I imagine she didn't tell you that we had a falling out due to an ideological difference and then she turned on me. Once she understood that she could not take me down in combat, she reached a deal with me: I'd spare her in exchange for her destroying her own regalia.*

So much for Gwalchmei Bears Lilies. *How did she do that to a proxy?*

Ze bites off half the protein bar. *An override, how else? If I were you, I wouldn't trust Recadat. To do this to your own regalia is an act of terrible perfidy.*

Never mind that Ouru drove her to it in the first place, though I can see what ze means. A point of honor: your life or your regalia's. Then again Gwalchmei merely lost a proxy, not his entire existence— the disparity in risk between duelist and regalia is enormous. I press zer for more details on the loser's fate, but ze is not forthcoming, busying zerself with zer little meal. All ze offers is, *Try the Gallery.*

We land in good time. Cadenza is a city of gnarled obsidian spires and high robed walls, bracketed by a body of water that brachiates across the ground. Briars and orchids drape the balconies and walkways, striping the streets in green shadows. The Divide system informs me that the sub-contest will begin within the day but nothing more specific. I keep an eye on the duelist and regalia counts, and keep my hand ready on the draw. I'm more vulnerable to attacks than ever, and I have already revealed myself as a duelist while on the shuttle.

The rule against bringing your regalia doesn't forbid me to stay within a certain radius of you, comes Daji's voice. *In fact, that rule doesn't kick in until you enter the arena proper. I'm watching over you, Detective. In case you get the idea of debauching some pretty young thing in Cadenza.*

"I have standards," I murmur under my breath. Cadenza's denizens have a look I can only call swampy—stooped by the indignities of living in this place, perpetually damp, with hair that makes me think of marsh weeds. The climate here is horrendously humid.

The arena could be anywhere—from the city map I would guess either the stadium in the center or the megastructure in Cadenza's eastern half, an enormous edifice that looms almost as high as the skeletal beasts beyond the walls. I stroll about, sticking to places with good cover where I won't be easy mark for a sniper. Ouru could make another attempt.

A storefront draws my eye. Mostly antiques, with one panel devoted to jewelry: elaborate crowns and necklaces of dynastic designs, tiny void jewelry settings, miniature tableaus made from semiprecious stones and ivory. What catches my attention is a single fire opal. Six point five carats, according to my overlays, suspended in a little cube without any setting. It reminds me of Eurydice. This would have been to her tastes.

On impulse—not quite yet knowing what for—I purchase the fire opal. The price is not low, but the proprietor is excited with the Vatican bracelet, and in the end I have to pay little.

I exit the shop to find Recadat waiting for me. Reliably punctual: she didn't board the same shuttle I did—she would've been recognized by Ouru and the rest—and so she arrived later, but not by much. She cuts a spare figure beneath a spread of orchids, a single point of efficiency amidst the tropical excess. When I teased her about being popular with women, I meant it—she has the needlepoint look of a stiletto, the trim glistening threat of something slender and utterly deadly. My opposite. When we first got to know each other I was surprised at how squeamish she could be in her philosophy and naivety, because on the field she was savagely competent. Tiger-spirited, almost a different person.

When she looks up, her gaze zeroes in on my purchase. "Who's that for?" The question is surprisingly sharp before it softens into something more playful: "You *did* pick up a woman! I knew it."

"It's just some bauble. I might wish to look at a fine object in my spare time." I put the fire opal away. "We should get moving."

Wonsul's voice sounds in my ear promptly, directing me toward the megastructure. He specifies the route and adds that any deviation from it will disqualify me. Sensible: each duelist will receive their own instruction, such that our paths will never cross before we reach the arena. I nod to Recadat. She will not enter the sub-contest, but will provide me with support. No part of the rules forbids such cooperation.

Up close, the place is even larger than it looked from above, the dimensions of it so gargantuan that the entire block is cast in jade shadow. Overgrowth swathes the banked walls and the bent columns, frothing out of cracked stone like ichor. I enter through a little gate Wonsul points me to.

It shuts behind me. Past that awaits a cavernous chamber and a single cage; inside the cage, a child of ten or twelve. Sedated. A first-aid kit lies on the ground.

"Duelists." Wonsul's voice emits from everywhere, every nook and cranny serving as his mouthpiece. "Be informed that this arena is not a sanctuary zone. One of you will have found a child. That shall be your objective: to win, bring her to the arena's center. If you lose her or eliminate her yourself, you forfeit the contest. If you leave the arena's bounds, you forfeit the contest. As with all other ceremonies, this is a duel to the death; all means may be utilized to achieve your goals, outside of using your regalia. May victory find you."

I open the first-aid kit and fish out a neutralizing tab. Keeping the child—almost certainly an AI proxy piloted by Wonsul's Exegesis—unconscious would minimize mess, but I have nothing I can fashion into a sling, and fighting one-handed is suicidal. To make sure of all my options, I heft the child up: light enough for me to carry, should it come to that. The kit also contains a sedative patch, in case I need to put her back to sleep. Considerate.

The override Recadat transferred me offers three options: *Retribution*, which calls down an orbital strike. *Seer*, which gives me access to satellites that would let me map the area and monitor other participants for a few minutes. The final option is labeled simply *Bulwark*. It requires triple-factor authentication—from myself, and the rest from my regalia. Daji doesn't answer when I inquire.

No jamming in the area. I pluck from my belt a tiny casket and pour out a handful of swarmbots no larger than poppy seeds. They fleet through cracks in the stone, and in a moment I have a visual of my part of the arena. Recadat's overlays hail mine and we establish a synchronization link: she's brought her own scouts and their view expand mine as they spread and cover more ground. The arena is densely but haphazardly built, seraphinite-colored chambers stacked on top of each other, connected by the occasional stairway and passage. I've been put into one of the lower levels and the openings and gaps between floors means I'll be easy pickings for duelists who have entered through one of the higher tiers.

My destination is a round little gazebo, accessible by two narrow catwalks exposed to the elements and also to other duelists. One of whom is heading toward me. I don't see Ouru; ze must be in a part of the arena my bots and Recadat's haven't reached yet.

The first duelist coming for me is a short, stocky man situated several levels above. Well-armed and evidently equipped with reconnaissance gear similar to mine. Reckless: he doesn't anticipate that other contestants would have scouted the area too.

He's climbing down a ladder when a shot takes him out. Precisely placed: it enters the back of his skull and punches cleanly through the medulla oblongata. Consciousness shuts down nearly instantly—a painless way to go, but looks ignoble all the same. Comical almost, how the muscles spasm in its last throes, how the collapse looks more like a puppet's than a person's.

The count of active duelists ticks down. Seventeen.

I open the cage, retrieve the child, and administer the tab that'll flush out the sedative. She comes awake with a jerk and a cough—convincing, for an AI proxy. When she meets my eyes, her gaze is vacant. I don't let Recadat view my visual feed. She's soft and would err on the side of assuming that this is a human child.

"On your feet," I say. The child obeys. Good; the AI has decided to spare me play-acted hysterics. "You're to follow me. Closely. Can you do that?"

She nods. I don't have sensors with biotelemetry functions, though a proxy can emulate human vital signs in any case—the only way to know for sure is to cut the chassis open. Her movements are stiff and heavy. That will be an issue.

I venture out the corridor, keeping an eye on what my scouts are sending me. I take a stairway and ascend without event, the child in tow. I can avoid the other duelists, though not for long. Two are directly above me, moving in parallel passages so that when I exit into the open air—a natural chokepoint—they'd be flanking me.

You doing all right in there, Thannarat? Recadat's frown is almost perceptible through the connection, even though we share no visual except the bots'.

Fine, considering. Keep expanding our range. The bots can do more than scout. As I move toward the chokepoint, I direct a stream of them toward one of the duelists, a wide-hipped man. Some cyborgs with military-grade defenses have personal dampener fields that'd have shorted out the bots; this person is not one of them. My swarmers streak into his ears and nose, puncture the wet surface tension of an eyeball and release a vitreous flood. The human face is a vulnerable entryway, full of unprotected orifices. Each offers up an open channel to the gossamer barrier of the meninges, the trembling isthmuses of cranial nerves, the artful whorls of the cerebrum. A little time in forensics is worth years of medical education. Mathematics and physics too, for fluid travel and splatter vectors—projecting where the blood will land after a gunshot, a knife slash, a switchblade stab. Everything has its own signature.

As soon as I emerge, I shoot almost without looking—I know the other duelist's exact position. He topples over screaming, one knee shattered. I fire again and he turns quiet. The counter ticks down once more: fifteen.

Ouru and Ensine Balaskas are the only known quantities here, and I have yet to encounter the latter. I still haven't seen Ouru, and I've expended some scouts; they now cover much less ground. I send the ones remaining ahead of me. Recadat's bots are a little more sluggish, hovering near the arena's periphery.

A different connection blinks on. *You pilot these things well, Detective, for a human. A specialty?*

I have a minor affinity for machines. The path is clear for the next couple stairways; good enough. *I thought our regalia aren't meant to interfere or assist.*

Daji laughs in my ear, lover-close. *I'm offering commentary, who'll chastise me for that? My help doesn't come so easily.*

Get too tart, I tell her, *and when I return to the Vimana I'll chastise you well enough.* Because this is what she wants to hear, the expected retort in the script she's set up between us. Her the petulant, flighty seductress in need of a firm hand.

Oh, you know just what to say; I've picked the right duelist. But don't let the thought of disciplining me distract you.

A segment of my swarmbots extinguishes, but not before I catch the visual—Ouru. I don't have enough scouts left to replace those, but I can now approximate zer location and trajectory. Not coming my way but moving to the center. Ze lacks my recon tools and, most likely, means to find a spot near the gazebo where ze can snipe down any approaching opponent.

The child stumbles behind me. Hefting her up I put her on my back and say, "Hold onto me. Your legs too." To my fortune, the child weighs no more than fifty kilos. Practically featherweight and my hands remain free. Still she adds bulk and disturbs my balance. Not my first time with a small person slung on my back, all the same. I keep up my pace, staying beneath the cover of foliage and slanted boulders.

Recadat's scouts spot a duelist sighting me down. I duck—the child slides off me; she'll be safe enough on the ground—and return fire. Bullets ping off stone.

Ouru chooses that moment to fry my swarmers, shutting down my view of the gazebo. I swear through my teeth, but I'll soon be there—

Daji's roses blaze in the corner of my vision. *Detective. Get out of there. Now.*

I don't ask questions; she would not send a message like this without cause. I hoist the child into my arms and start running back the way I came. A shot cracks above me and another; one grazes my shoulder but I don't slow down—the time for assessing damage will be later. For now the point is to *have* a later.

My trajectory is not ideal. I stare down a crumbled walkway and take a running leap, landing on the other side more heavily than I'd like: the floor dents and the tiles creak.

I'm clear of the arena, ninety meters out, when light lances down the sky. The orbital strike is surgical. The heat of it singes my cheeks and buffets my hair; when it is over afterimages strobe across my retinas.

On the ground the child stirs and twitches. It is when her gaze clears and she starts screaming that I realize I have been carrying a flesh-and-blood creature, human and not an AI proxy after all. In the Divide module, the count of duelists has dropped to eleven.

Wonsul's Exegesis picked up the child before I departed Cadenza; her parents had agreed, evidently, to sacrifice her to the contest in exchange for accelerated entry into Shenzhen Sphere. So much for the nobility of parental love. Still, the girl's alive; sometimes that's all you can ask for.

Unfortunately the overseer does not agree to hand me an override even if I'm the de facto winner. Recadat is safe, if shaken. Nothing quite like this has happened so far during this round of the Divide. She stayed behind in Cadenza to see if she can find out who engaged the Retribution command.

The graze on my shoulder proves merely cosmetic, an unlovely scratch on artificial shell but nothing more, and I return to Libretto without incident.

Once I'm in the Vimana suite I breathe more easily—it is a false illusion, but habit situates the human mind to regard a base, a temporary residence, as refuge. I toss my coat aside and settle down on a divan.

Daji glides behind me, sliding cool hands onto my shoulders. "I can almost smell your adrenaline," she says in my ear. "It's piquant. Welcome home, Detective."

I inhale—Daji smells of roses and pomegranates. Olfactory

emitters, customizable to any fragrance. From my pocket I bring out the box from the antique shop. "This is for you."

A rustle as she removes it from its paper lining. "Close your eyes." I comply; after a few seconds she murmurs, "Now open them."

I do to the sight of Daji kneeling between my legs, dressed once more in that scantiness of pelts and petals. The fire opal gleams between her collarbones, embedded into her chassis. It looks right at home, complementing the shades of her flower-and-fox raiment. She has placed one of her hands on my thigh. Her other holds a prosthesis—mine; she must've been cataloguing the contents of my suitcase.

"Let me," she says, "take care of you."

My breath hitches. She is right that I'm still fresh from the fight, blood coursing with the near-miss of that orbital strike. To narrowly escape your mortality gives quick spice to the libido, and this would be such an easy way to extinguish those inconvenient embers I carry for Recadat. "You're a proxy."

"That does not mean I lack. Quite the opposite. In me you'll find all that you need, my duelist." She leans a little closer. "I've been so patient. Should I not be rewarded a little? Should you not indulge yourself so your humors will be soothed, your hungers sated? Then you'll be ready for the rest. The Divide is a taxing campaign."

"And duelist and regalia should be wedded in intent and action, so I have heard." A split second's decision that I may later regret. For the moment I can only think of how soft her skin looks, how voluptuous she is, the banquet offered by her breasts. Those indentations of clavicles framing the fire opal. I take off one glove and cup her face, running my thumb along jawline and then earlobe. Utterly authentic. I'd never know I am with a machine.

Daji grins, her teeth showing sharp and fine and ravenous. She unbuckles my belt then replaces it with the harness that secures the prosthesis to me. I activate the module associated with it, the sensory array that joins my nervous system to the device: a thick length of supple material, done in oxblood. Once it is affixed and online, it rests between my legs, soft.

Her fingers graze slowly along the shaft, stroking, teasing. It stiffens. "Sensitive," she says. "This responds to your arousal, doesn't it? Most appliances of this category are more . . . static."

I rub my thumb against her lips. Feels, briefly, the tips of her incisors. Little needlepoints. "This stays hard as long as I have the will."

"A lovely function." Her hand encircles the device, taking hold, running up and down: exploring its contours, its dimensions. She breathes onto its tip. Her tongue darts out, but does not touch. "How virile you are, Detective."

My nipples are hard, painful points. Hers too—what she wears does not cover much, though for the moment it gives modesty to her lower half. Her skull feels delicate in my palm, avian, made for a creature of aerodynamics and endless expanses. "Enough talking, Daji. Show me what you're made for."

She places her hands on my thighs and takes the length between her lips, nearly all of it at once. An impossible feat for most human partners, the piece being considerable in dimensions—her mouth is endlessly capacious. She works the prosthesis as though it is her favorite instrument, her attention a thing of arias and complex maneuvers. My breathing serrates as her teeth put pressure on the most sensitive points. My vision brightens. I dig my fingers into her scalp and can tell from her quickened pace that this is exactly what she likes, how she wants to be handled, the fulcrum of her desire. Machine, yes. Not without her preferences, all the same.

It doesn't take long before I convulse and fill her mouth with a substance the color and consistency of thick wine. Daji swallows it all, lapping it up as though it's the most precious liquor this side of the galaxy.

"The profile of good sangria," she says. "Your taste is good *and* you taste excellent."

I exhale. "We're far from done."

"Yes, I can tell, this is still hard—"

While I may be no judge of AIs, I am a good judge of women. So I am confident when I yank her up by the hair, close one hand around her throat, and growl, "You do like it rough, don't you."

Her eyelashes beat rapidly. Part black, part gold. Subtly dichroic. "This you call rough, Detective?"

I use her neck as a handhold to drag her to her feet and fling her onto the bed: enough force to knock the wind out of her, if she was a non-augmented human. She lies very still, her hands flat against the cerise sheets that bunch and crease around her like stricken lilies.

"I can accommodate *any* desire," Daji purrs, her eyes brilliant. "In the most literal sense. My anatomy—it can be anything you want."

"Give me a cunt," I say, pulling off the pelt that covers her waist and hip.

What appears at first blank—mannequin neutrality—shifts and reflows, rearranging itself into that familiar part, one of my favorite sights on a partner. I should be unsettled; instead this thrills me, the strangeness of it, the display of machine finesse. She's given herself the gorgeous folds of labia, the unmistakable clitoral nub as hard as a pearl. Comprehensive in detail, a locus where basal urges intersect. I can smell her heat, her salt.

My left hand on the back of her neck. My right on her wrist, wrenching it so far back that on a human her elbow might have snapped or dislocated. But she's strong, a body of numinous might, impossible for me to damage. Daji is a canvas that will never tear no matter the force of the pen, the searing of the ink.

I lower myself and push into her with the most minimal of resistance. She is slick, a furnace, far hotter than her mouth. Her inside caresses my prosthesis, nearly as dexterous as her fingers. The world tunnels down to sensation, to the motions of her juddering like a rag doll beneath me, to the bed shaking under us like tectonic prayer. Several times I fill her, flip her over, fill her again.

When I withdraw from her I am panting, my limbic architecture sundered by the song of her, my mind reconstituting piece by piece. She levers herself up, meeting my eyes, flushed. Her lower lip is swollen and bleeding—she must have bitten it.

"If we had unlimited time," I whisper, "I'd be fucking your mouth again."

There is no airiness in her laugh: it is deep, smoky, onyx and oodh.

"We do have a lot of time. Not unlimited though; who has eternity? Not even the Mandate itself. You were wonderfully rough. A human would be incredibly sore right about now, but I'm not one of those, so we are a most perfect match." Her hand slides up my thigh, to the silk shirt which has come loose and gaping. "The whole of you makes an interesting artistic perspective from down here. Every square millimeter of you is so pleasing."

I drop to the bed; we lie facing each other. My own cunt is engorged, sensitive. "Do you often do this?" I fit my hand into her lumbar curve, half-expecting to find it gone to metal and silicon. But it stays flesh-like, deceptively organic. A few roses susurrate under my fingers.

"Do what? Have a good time?" Daji rubs the base of the prosthesis. My nervous system rings staccato with each touch. "Tell me, Detective. Does the fact I'm a proxy add to the appeal? Do you find the synthetic fascinating, the alloyed skin more alluring than skin that is not?"

"You're well aware that your chosen looks are breathtaking. A woman hardly needs to have such . . . specific predilections to want to push you up against the wall and make you scream." I pinch one bare breast. She arches into me, as reactive as a taut wire. "But perhaps."

Her lips purse on the thumb of my free hand. She talks around it as she might around a cigarette. "I can tell a fetish when I see it—the alacrity of your orgasms. The vigor. Not that I mind; some humans are ashamed of wanting a proxy and it's a waste of everyone's time."

"So you've tried other humans before."

"Possessive," she says, pleased. "It's just that I don't enjoy inter-course between my own kind, whereas what we just did together? That's exactly what I crave. Exquisite. Addictive. And you're so honest about your wants."

I run my nail over her jaw; I suspect that even if I try to break skin, I would leave no marks, or no marks that won't heal within minutes. My thumb reaches the choker around her throat. I pull. The choker snaps. Beneath it, her throat is a vision. "Is your preference common among AIs?"

"Not at all, though most of my peers don't care who I choose to pursue. A few are prudes and would tell you I'm sick. Why, does it bother you that you just fucked a machine pervert?"

"Hardly. You and I are both perverts." I kiss the back of her hand, repeating that gesture that sealed our pact. "I assume Wonsul didn't take issue with you giving me a warning. Seeing that you were able to monitor overrides."

"Retribution is a rather blatant command. A human could've seen an oncoming orbital strike with the naked eye. Wonsul cannot fault me for using my optics."

Except she warned me well before it landed. The Retribution armament, being Mandate equipment, would be cutting-edge. There would have been no telltale prelude to a discharge, and certainly not that far ahead. "How much is a regalia supposed to see into the Divide system?"

"Walls are permeable things. For any destination there are a hundred thousand roads to it. Every rule is made to be bent. That's how the game is played." Daji taps my nose. "Now, the real reason you joined the Court of Divide."

Sex where I don't need to hold back has a strange effect on me. The aftermath of it wildly varies; for intimacy to be its immediate consequence is rare. I might tell her anything. "I came from Ayothaya." Her weight shifts on the mattress as she twines herself closer to me, one thigh slipping between mine. As if she can't get enough of me, or a good pretense of such. "My life there was unremarkable—I worked as a detective with public security and went freelance after I realized the force inflicted violence to the guiltless more than it prevented. Not because I'm some altruist. I dislike senselessness."

"*When we shear the world in half, we demarcate with great precision: those who wield themselves like a knife and those who wield themselves like a whip.*" She nods. "This is an inexact quote—it comes from a meditation on violence, a text one of my duelists liked. You belong to the taxonomy of the blade; violence may excite you, but you don't strike indiscriminately."

My mouth quirks. "I don't know about that. In any case, I could find all the thrill I wanted working for myself and did well enough at it to prosper. During all this I had a wife, and our marriage . . . There was a gulf that kept widening until we could no longer bridge the difference. It wasn't the nature of my job—that never bothered her. But she felt I lacked . . . that I couldn't show properly that I loved her, to the point she couldn't tell if I loved her at all."

Her hand slips under my shirt and comes to rest on a breast. One of her roses caresses my stomach; I was right that they're part of her, appendages as mobile as her fingers. "I disagree. You're perfectly good at showing how you feel."

"No, Eurydice had the right of it. I was a fool. And then she caught wind of the haruspex initiative." Haruspices: the composites that live on Shenzhen Sphere, sacred cyborgs who are half human and half AI—two beings, one body. "She had a lifelong fascination with machines; we had that in common. Once the haruspex initiative opened to outside applicants, she divorced me and left for Shenzhen."

"Heartless," Daji whispers.

"She did what was right for herself. I was—" Disconsolate, because I was selfish; because I wanted things to continue as they were, comfortable for me and unbearable for her. "A few years later, I was contacted by the Mandate. Their representative let me know that Eurydice had listed me as her next of kin and that the haruspex process had failed. That nothing of her was left except a copy of her neural stacks and genetic information. The day after, a queen's ransom materialized in my account. I was going to send it back, but it turned out there was no source. The money just showed up as though it'd always been there, as though that was any kind of compensation. The Mandate didn't respond to my demands for Eurydice's data. I never heard from an AI again."

"Until you met Benzaiten?"

"The Hellenes decimated our military, executed our commanders and ministers, and charred a good amount of our infrastructure. There's a Hellenic governor installed there now, sitting in our capital. Citizens are interdicted from leaving—I got out because I had the means and the contacts and the wealth. Most didn't." My mouth twitches. Not exactly a smile, more a rictus. "Benzaiten came to me while I was on a ship, bound for nowhere important. Xe told me about Septet, knowing that I'd be motivated to enter the Divide either way— by the invasion or by the . . . by what happened to my ex-wife. Why xe singled me out I wouldn't begin to guess. Some machine caprice."

Daji drums her fingertips on my nipple. Her roses tickle my ribcage. "I'm a machine and I'm capricious, so I shouldn't take offense. Well, which is it? The Hellenes or your ex-wife?"

"Eurydice," I say at once. For so long I've mourned her. Grief is an irrevocable beast: it can eat and eat until the meat and gristle are cleaned from the bones, and then it'll crush the bones and swallow them down. I've fought it for years. I intend to conquer it at last.

She stiffens. "You're a woman motivated by passion above all. I shouldn't be surprised. The subjugation of your homeworld doesn't offend you?"

"It does. Who knows—before the end I may change my mind." Recadat's idealism against my self-interest.

"If you choose war, Detective, I'll personally accompany you to Ayothaya and settle the score. A whole warship of me. Their troops will fall before me like walls of dust."

"An extravagant offer." I gather a handful of her hair and inhale. Still rose and pomegranate, tinged with sangria. A notification blinks in the corner of my vision. The Vimana's. "Let me get the door." I unclasp the harness and leave the prosthesis in Daji's keeping—she raises an eyebrow and murmurs something about remote access. The fox climbs onto my shoulder.

There's no one at the door; on the floor is a sealed envelope, black striped with gold. The suite's security feed shows me that no one has been in this part of the corridor. An AI must have made the delivery.

I open the door partway. The fox trots out to retrieve the envelope and returns with the paper in its mouth. *Nothing explosive or toxic that I can detect,* says Daji. *No anti-cybernetic payload, no anything that could harm you. From material composition this appears to be plain paper. Black ink: carbon, solvent, surfactant, the usual.*

All the same I put on my gloves before touching the thing. Conventional adhesive. Perfectly good paper, the envelope stiff and the letter within thick and sumptuous. Neat handwriting; Cyrillic script. My overlays translate: *Felicitations to the late-coming duelist partnered to the regalia of roses. I am sure you know who I am—my reputation must precede me. Unlike most who join the Court of Divide I have no wish, save to pursue the purest form of conversation: combat. I sense that you have instincts not unlike mine, a connoisseur of the soldier's ataraxia. Let us meet honestly and test ourselves, duelist against duelist and regalia against regalia. I've attached a place and time.*

Yours, Ensine Balaskas.

&

Recadat meets her lover in a dining orchard where pollen glitters like gold and tourmaline, and the air is redolent with frangipani and persimmons. Foliage both true and artificial cups the restaurant in a palm of boughs and canopies, though they don't entirely mask Cadenza's hot, muddy stench. Her lover's table perches on a stretch of obsidian that juts out from the building's flank, and though there are railings—translucent, barely visible—she feels as she sits down that they're at the edge of a precipice, a vast plummet. Sixteen floors aboveground and fatal.

Her lover has already started in on their meal. The cut of meat on their plate is so raw that it rests in a puddle of its own death, like fresh kill, and they're cutting slices so thin and fine that it should not be possible with a table knife. They lift one morsel to their mouth, swallow it whole. The meat is tender, well-marbled, glistening with blood and marinade. Salt, she guesses, and flecks of spice she does not recognize. The dish is as far from Ayothayan cuisine as it can be.

"Have you had a good outing?" They lick a red blot off their full lips. Today they've painted their mouth the shade of graphite. "What good fortune that you weren't there when the arena was struck."

"Did you do it?"

A small chuckle—it rings the mesh of chimes they wear like sealing talismans around their throat. "You know I didn't. I would never harm a woman who occupies so much of your thought."

"She doesn't—"

They take hold of Recadat's wrist, a fingernail in duochrome digging into her flesh. Not painful. Enough to interrupt her sentence. "What news from Ayothaya?"

She composes herself. "Another town burned. Someone had the bright idea to try armed resistance. That didn't go well, the Hellenes outgunned them completely." And are not prone to leniency. She wishes she could have told the insurgents to choose differently; to coordinate with other efforts, to bear with the state of atrocity. To wait. She wishes she could send secret messages, but Septet is closed to outside networks. The only news she can get from Ayothaya is via Mandate-sanctioned information brokers, coming neither cheap nor fast.

"Detective Thannarat didn't give you updates?"

"She must have made detours before coming here, to get prepped and armed, to gather everything she'd need for Septet. Her information's no more recent than mine."

Her lover spears another slice of meat, this one thicker, the shape of it making her think of a tongue. They eat the morsel immaculately. "Do you really believe that? Does she behave or sound like a patriot?"

Recadat brushes an insect off her sleeve. A gnat. There was an excess of mosquitoes where she came from, and she used to have a phobia as a child that extended to all bugs: the way their bodies could release unseen horrors, pustulent liquid and larvae and egg sacs. Insect promiscuity. Her cheeks itch. "You don't have to be a patriot to want a home to go back to."

"It is true that you've known her for so long while I don't know her at all, except through your accounting. My judgment of her character could be incorrect." They empty their long-stemmed glass in a single draw and still make that look surgical rather than sloppy. "Yet she doesn't strike me as driven by a sense of home. What you and she have come here to do requires that you're ready to confront the limits of your mortal coil. My impression, however, is that she has nothing in particular to return to, no piece of Ayothaya she'd die to preserve. What do you think?"

"Of course she does. Everyone has something." But if pressed, she wouldn't be able to name any for Thannarat other than Eurydice, and that's gone. She admired that in her senior partner, that core of absolute independence, unburdened by attachment. No place for softness, no chink in the armor. A force of nature more than a human being.

"A world is so little, Recadat. What matters is passion. That is what propels people to great deeds, to terrible carnage. To hate or love is the true fuel behind human motive. You'll immolate yourself for it and march forward even as you burn."

In the link she shares with her lover, images unfold: life-size, so that in her vision their table is suddenly surrounded by a battalion of Thannarat. Some clothed, others much less so. The hard bulk of her, the physique of a mountain, unyielding and permanent: Thannarat's back makes her think of boulders. Even the bare shoulders captivate— the potency they promise, the suggestion of what she is capable of. Recadat wrenches her gaze away from a glimpse of wiry hair between two thick thighs ridged with cybernetic connectors. "Stop that."

"They're approximations. Did I err in my extrapolation of her musculoskeletal structure? Perhaps she has more scars, interesting ones that arrest your eyes? You could show me your own simulacra. Over the years you must've made several for private use, imbued them with rudimentary heuristics and linked them to your sensory arrays. To simulate what it might be like to lie with the woman you long for the most."

"I've done no such thing." Completely disrespectful, utterly violating. She never even considered it.

"My poor Recadat," they murmur, dismissing Thannarat's doppel-gangers, "not even an outlet for all that pent-up frustration. It's not as if you are sworn to chastity, given everything you let me do to you in bed and how much you enjoy it, the sounds you make—"

"Stop *that*," Recadat says again, cheeks blistering. The nearest table is far away enough that she hopes they didn't overhear. Two young people, a couple she thinks, one in tuxedo and the other in an adapted hanfu. Excellent tailoring; she would know, having invested a good deal in her own wardrobe. On Septet marks of wealth are ubiquitous—signifiers of poverty are confined to border residences—but there is no real commerce beyond tourist attractions. She can't make sense of the world's economy, if it even has one. All of it seems pantomimed. "Have you found more duelists? I've been busy."

Her lover refills their glass, seemingly just so they can swirl it, that liquor the sumptuous color of brass. They peer at her over the wine-wet rim. "Why do you think I asked to meet here? The table behind you—the one in the tuxedo—that is a duelist. He is without a regalia. Nevertheless it's best to cull the herd, wouldn't you agree. The fewer pieces on the board, the cleaner things shall be."

"Do you want to shadow him or shall I?" She's done that so many times on Septet. As if her career in public security never ended, a seamless continuation. Stalking a suspect. Stakeouts.

Their eyes widen. "Why? You can kill him where he sits. It saves so much time and we have such a long list to work our way down."

Recadat glances at that table. Situated far enough they cannot eavesdrop: that has different significance now. Neither the supposed duelist nor his companion appears threatening, though she knows that is deceptive. Duelists can be anyone, look like anything. "In broad daylight?"

"This is Septet, my jewel. All violence is permitted. Everyone has agreed to death and ought to defend themselves accordingly, take the appropriate precautions. Who sits down to dine unarmed? You'd never be so complacent. Detective Thannarat wouldn't be either. Oh, think of this as helping *her*."

"I'm not going to just walk over and shoot someone in the head."

"You can sit right here and shoot him in the head, Recadat. The range is nothing and you've got perfectly outstanding aim."

Recadat's breath scrapes through her teeth. Her lover has not yet been wrong, has singled out duelists with the unerring precision of a hawk. She looks at the remains of their meal, now reduced to a thin smear, every shred of meat put away. "And his companion?"

"She's an ordinary Septet citizen, insofar as this place has a citizenry."

The pair is twenty-two, twenty-five at most—practically

adolescent. She can hardly remember being that young. Her hope is that they are not related or in love: it's easier to carry this out if she imagines they are coworkers, casual acquaintances, something brief and impermanent. Few tables in the orchard are filled, and she knows neither patrons nor staff will stop her. There's no public security here, no authority to appeal to. Wonsul's Exegesis will intervene only if Divide rules are being broken. Homicide is beyond his jurisdiction or, she suspects, his interest. What do machines care for morals or human lives.

Despite everything, she's never committed such an act. That she has the capability is not in question: she dislikes violence and yet has found herself prodigious at it. Adrenaline suspends her doubt, enables her to do what is necessary in the moment even if afterward she might regret it. But on Septet there is no social contract; there is only the savage demand of the Divide, the reduction of people to feral beasts.

Recadat gets up. She strides to the table, and once she's close both the man and woman look up at her, startled—perplexed. There is no hint of recognition in his face that she's a threat, and he still looks surprised when the muzzle of her gun enters his field of vision. The impact of the shot sends him reeling back. Instantly gone. The human skull is not designed to withstand such force, and he appears unaugmented.

His companion screams, scrambling away as blood leaks and soaks the table, its spotless cloth, the meal they've just shared. Escargot and foie gras, plated with a truly fine eye, postmodern and architectural. All those tessellated layers. She thinks of leaving a large tip, a compliment to the chef.

The woman flees. The other tables are now empty. They know what is going on, and that there is no recourse: to stay is to risk a duelist's bloodthirst, and they would assume she has her regalia about. She holsters her gun, stepping away from the corpse, and waits for the duelist count to go down.

A full minute passes. The count stays at eleven. Impossible—the system updates within seconds, if not the very moment the duelist's brain terminates and the final shred of consciousness succumbs.

Recadat stands there, turning cold as her lover sidles up behind her, placing a snakeskin-gloved hand in the small of her back.

"My bad," they purr against her neck. "Even I make mistakes, jewel. But it is as I said, everyone who lives on Septet consents to this potential fate. Don't think anything of it. No one is going to. Are you hungry? Let me treat you; I trust the kitchen staff hasn't evacuated."

CHAPTER FOUR

The air in the gym is frigid, and few other guests are about. Various machines line the sides, several resembling torture contraptions and medical cradles more than they do exercise instruments. Privacy spheres veil several. The space is so wide, all paneled wood and a floor-to-ceiling glass wall, that no one needs to be within twenty meters of each other if they don't want to—which is how I prefer it. I attract no particular attention as I go through warm-up routines: in some places baring your chest in public is risqué or criminal, but Septet is not one of them.

I work my arms and shoulders until they're supple, until my rotator cuffs and ulnas turn like well-oiled cogs and my muscles run as warm as a faultless engine. There is a careful balance to strike when most of one's body is cybernetics—the organic parts must also be maintained, and there's only so much my nanites can do. Metabolism, maintenance of the viscera, streamlining somatic processes. But to stay in fighting trim I still need to contribute my part.

The pull-up machine registers my body mass as I touch it, adjusting for my muscle index and my cybernetic-to-organic ratio. I grip the bar overhead, adjust my form, and begin. In my former profession, officers often prioritized their legs, but for recreation I've found it most satisfying to pit myself against gravity. The line of exertion I can feel clearly down my arms, shoulders, spine; my entire body works and bends itself to this one single goal. I pull. I pull until my feet are off the ground, and hold. Half a minute before I lower myself. The next time I hold a little longer, until I do so for a full minute in the air, aloft only by the power of my hands and arms. It demands the entire apparatus of the body, it stretches every tendon. Ascend, descend. Unnecessary thoughts recede: endorphins cleanse the mind, leaving my senses and perception with the clarity of new glass, of a clear morning.

I move on to leg lifts: less strenuous, since from the knees down I'm cybernetic. By the time I'm done, sweat soaks my breasts and stomach, collecting in the crooks of my elbows, the backs of my knees. Nanites flood through my augmentation couplings, lowering temperature where the pseudoskin doesn't vent excess heat.

Daji brings me towels and a tray of drinks. She's gone out of her way to put on a Vimana uniform, though her version is a little less modest—the neckline plunges deeper, the hemline floats shorter. Maroon stockings, burnished with hints of copper, sheathe her legs. "You're such a vision," she murmurs as she wipes me down, lingering on the dark seams where flesh blends into musculoskeletal couplings. "Do you suppose I could clean up all this salt with my tongue? It seems wasted on towels."

"This is a little public. And my sweat contains trace coolant." Not that she'd have issue ingesting that. The drinks she brought are chilled tea: assam, oolong, ceylon. I sip from each cup. Strong and fragrant, richly flavored, each full of bitter complexity. "I'm surprised you brought me such sober things, not cocktails."

"I considered that but I got distracted when I found coconut rum in your suite's sideboard." She wrinkles her nose. "I thought of throwing it out, but on the off chance that you might enjoy such a freakish and unlovely concoction . . . "

The idea an AI would have such specific dislikes amuses me. "And here I thought I was going to have you lap it up from between my thighs." Half-teasing. I don't know, yet, what to do about intimacy with Daji. Whether it should continue, whether I should indulge myself and her. I'm tending toward yes. Daji is less complicated than Recadat.

"Even for such a treat I'll not stoop to coconut-flavored anything. I *can* make parts of my proxy dispense liquor, if you wish. I just need to learn what you like if I'm going to mix cocktails."

An image, incredibly vivid, flashes through my mind. Of drinking sake straight from her mouth, or vodka from between her breasts and other such outlandish things. I set down one of the cups and put my knuckles under her chin. "My regalia. You're such a hungry little thing."

"Exclusively for you." Daji's hand strokes my bicep, circles around to my back; she cups her palm over a shoulder blade. "Look at you. Your musculature is made to be serviced by my mouth. In prehistoric times you'd be thought a demigod, a hero born of woman and divine flame."

"And you're an immortal seductress out of myth. The populace would throw themselves into boiling cauldrons if it'd amuse you. You would be declared the most gorgeous in all the land." I cradle her jawline. It's so easy to fall into this, to fall into her; more than that I *want* to. "Still would be; I like to think I'm a good judge of feminine beauty and no one I've ever met compares to you."

"Flatterer." But her smile is wide and genuine; guileless. Or it would be, if she were human. She sits down at my feet and puts her head on my thigh, heedless of the sweat-soaked fabric. I stroke her head as I would a pet, surveying the mostly-empty gym, wondering how much we could get away with.

Through the glass wall I spot a familiar figure stepping out to the pool—Ouru. Ze's in a nacreous bodysuit, midriff and ankles bared. Ze is slightly soft around the middle, pleasant to look at, zer lower half a runner's physique. Thighs and calves like the trunks of well-fed trees. Ze is not looking my way, though I have no doubt ze is aware of me. Zer regalia would be watching out for zer, as mine is.

Ouru must have warmed up elsewhere, for ze slips at once into the water. In there ze looks born to it, moving under the currents with naga elegance. I could imagine scales on zer, piscine gills.

"You're watching zer a little too intently, Detective." Daji rubs my knee. "I'm right here."

"Ze's not my type; too androgynous. It's useful to know the enemy, isn't that so?"

"You can study your enemy without staring at zer bare skin."

"There isn't much to see," I say mildly. "My appreciation of zer is entirely respectful."

I finish my tea. Ouru completes zer laps, gets out of the water, and stretches out beneath an enormous palm frond the color of crocoite. Our connection establishes and I'm pulled into zer virtuality.

When I join zer it is within the image of a Theravada temple, a prayer hall of convex gold ceiling and suspended paper talismans plated in silver. Several Buddhas, reclining or seated beneath bodhi trees with rose-gold and copper canopies. It may be cultural training—I attended temples not unlike this in my youth—but to me this speaks of spirituality far more sincerely than the Cenotaph and Wonsul's monk costume.

Ouru is waiting for me in the scriptorium, holding in zer hand a long, pleated scroll made of sapphire paper. Ze nods at me. "Thanks for being reasonable." Then, as if seeing me or rather my body's specifications for the first time, "You're mostly prosthetic. Is that by necessity or by choice?"

"I could take that as a very rude question." From one of the shelves I pluck a hand-bound volume: a theological text that addresses different, syncretic versions of the Siddhartha myth. One has him, the holy prince, as always having been an androgyne. "It's by choice. I could have had my limbs regrown, but I preferred cybernetics."

"Hell of an upkeep."

"Fine once you've acclimated; better if you have the means to ease the procedures." I nod at the virtual setting. "You're devout?"

"Yes. Just not the pacifistic kind. Judging by your name and accent, you must've grown up somewhere Theravada-majority as well." Ze folds up the scroll and returns it to its place. "You're working with Recadat, correct? I'm surprised she would let you talk to me. That's a single-minded young woman."

"What caused your falling out?"

Ouru's chuckle is like abacus beads. "She believed her need nobler than mine and that I ought to give way to her when the game has whittled down to the two of us. Each of us believes our cause is the most just or the most urgent, no? I regret that I ever gave her the impression I'd yield victory to her—I don't like parting ways in acrimony. But it is what it is."

I run my fingers over the volume in my hand, appreciating the fine detail: the textural arrays, the faint smell of old paper. "What's your goal, then?" The great wish, the desire that burns so bright in Ouru's soul that ze would risk zerself in unfathomable machine schemes.

"I could just not tell you. But it's no secret—I told Recadat. I'd like to become a haruspex."

Why is everyone obsessed with that, I wonder. The advantages are attractive enough now that—allegedly—the process has been perfected: no more botches like Eurydice. A haruspex is revered on Shenzhen, granted not just comfort but every available privilege. Access to the cutting edge of anti-agathic extension, as close to immortal as a human can get. That was one of the draws for Eurydice; she wanted to live forever. "Bypassing the usual petition process, including Shenzhen's prohibitive immigration control, I'm guessing."

"Precisely. The usual process—well, they take few applicants, the criteria are vague and nebulous. This way it's guaranteed." Ze gestures toward the far end of the scriptorium, at a window lit by an emerging sunrise. "I don't intend to lose. Under no circumstances will I forfeit. Do you understand, Khun Thannarat?"

At the window a figure coalesces, blue-black smoke solidifying into a silhouette and then a clear shape—Houyi's Chariot. My first good look at the regalia. Broad-shouldered and about my height, as Recadat said. Their face remains hidden, save for a visor through which their eyes burn like twin reactors.

"I admire when a person has a clear objective they work toward." I nod. "Ensine Balaskas has sent me her calling card."

"Then I anticipate you and your regalia will soon be destroyed. My condolences in advance."

"I wouldn't be so sure." My eyes remain on Houyi's Chariot, drawn to the outline of them limned by oil-slick corposant. "Not very talkative, are they?"

"Houyi talks when they deem the world fit to hear their voice." Ouru gives zer regalia a small fond smile. The expression transforms an unremarkable face into a tender portrait. "Now, you're going to ask for my cooperation against Ensine. My answer is no."

"My regalia is Empress Daji Scatters Roses Before Her Throne."

A small twitch from Houyi. "So she's back in the game, I didn't think she would join this round." Their voice is like a slow rockslide. "Ouru, consider her proposal. Daji is unusual."

Ouru lets out a soft huff, not quite a laugh. "Coming from you that is high praise. Nevertheless, there can only be one victor. I can't share the prize."

The regalia makes a small, inscrutable gesture. "Daji used to be a haruspex."

That I didn't anticipate, though it'd explain why my treasure of roses and pelts acts human so well—she used to share a body with one. Ouru widens zer eyes, expression turning thoughtful. Speculative.

"I'll ask her if she would vouch for your haruspex application," I offer Ouru. "Put it on the table, though I can't promise anything absolute. Houyi—what happens to regalia whose duelists have died or forfeited?"

For a moment I expect the AI would not answer. Then they say, "Unattached regalia may not engage in combat without being partnered to a duelist, and they may seek a new duelist to bind themselves to. Ouru and I have been eliminating a number of them."

Five regalia remain. Only two are unknown variables. "Can one duelist bind themselves to more than one regalia at a time?"

"Not without frying their brains." Houyi does not elaborate. "We'll be your allies, provisionally. Contingent on you convincing Daji to assist Ouru. And speaking of that, it'd be best if you leave now."

I start to ask. The virtuality's fabric starts to rip. Scriptorium shelves give way to blinding gold. Chun Hyang emerges wreathed in its own brilliance, and where its feet fall Ouru's virtuality singes and blackens. Houyi's Chariot steps between their duelist and the intruder, spear drawn.

No point staying and inquiring as to Ouru's operational security. I pull free of zer virtuality. Back in the gym, in a wash of synaptic storm: the physicality of a hard bench, the sunlight pouring in, and the water murmuring outside. The warm weight of Daji has annexed my lap.

"You were gossiping about me with Houyi." She bites my earlobe, none too gently. "Very rude, Detective Thannarat."

"I was implying that you were resplendent, without peer."

"And yet you were asking Houyi if you could have more than one regalia."

"As a hypothetical. I don't plan to adopt any. You're my only partner." I wrap my arm around her thick waist. "Your opinion on my little machinations?"

"Clever that you intuited naming me would make Houyi talk. They and I are friendly rivals, though I don't need their help to take down Chun Hyang." Her delicate shoulders rise and fall. "I've battled Chun Hyang's Glaive many times, across the rounds."

I trail one hand down her spine, languorous, appreciating each curve and bend. The architecture of vertebrae: brittle in a human body, impregnable in hers. "The records suggest Chun Hyang has won every round it entered."

She pinches my forearm. "The archivist is not a reliable narrator. What, you think we'd let him do this silly chronicling if his information was *accurate*? He's part of Septet's infrastructure. The papers he keeps have multiple versions."

I grimace; she laughs. "And you I am to take as reliable? Why make the Divide so deeply . . . difficult? The deceptions on deceptions, the double- and triple-crossing, the masquerades." Though I haven't yet met any human I'd suspect of being an AI, but *that* is the point. "The destabilizing of all aspirants and duelists."

"We didn't create this to make it easy for you to win, Detective. There have been rounds where it was all pyrrhic victory or scorched earth where not a single soul emerged in triumph. This game's for—" Her head cocks. "Aren't you going to ask about my time as a haruspex?"

Machines do not hesitate or misspeak. She's not going to tell me about the Divide's true aim, though I'm starting to glimpse the iceberg-tip of it. For now that's a suspicion only. I set the thought aside. "I'm interested in a different question, Daji. Duelists risk themselves in the Divide for tremendous gain. Why do machines bother? Individually, not the great overarching purpose of the Mandate. It can't be just to stave off boredom—this is too much investment."

"Says who? An AI can run a range of parallel threads, piloting scores of proxies. Even now I might be entertaining a dozen other lovers."

"I can hardly fault your appetite." I kiss her palm. "But I do aim to be your most interesting, such that when I occupy your attention I'll force you to tunnel down to, oh, five others. When we fuck, that's going to have to be down to two others at most. So what's the Divide to you? Personally?"

"Cocky." Daji squeezes my thigh. "On Shenzhen, where I was made, a haruspex is the incubator for new AIs. You meld with a human and, at the end of this life cycle, the human half dies and is sloughed off. For me—for us—we ran into a . . . neurological incompatibility early on that made it no longer possible for the haruspex to hold. One of us had to give. My human half chose to sacrifice herself so I could continue."

"I'm sorry."

"Don't be. In me she'll be immortal. I am her living memorial. But because our time was cut short, it gave me a peculiar longing; I don't think many AIs share it. I don't want to become a haruspex again, that was too limiting and I've been granted my full capacity since." She runs her nail up my throat, drawing circles until she reaches my cheek. "I want a companion, Detective. Someone who'll love and cherish me as my human half did. Someone who is mine, all mine, and who pleases me in all ways. The only one—once I've found this companion I will require no other. No more dalliances, no more diversions. Just her."

I smile, slight, against her thumb. "And have you found such a person?"

"I've come close once; now I come closer still. I stand on the brink." Her hand tightens on my jawline. "This time I don't intend to lose. I'll turn Septet to cinders if I need to. Victory, Detective, at any cost."

☒

By late night I send Ouru a message; ze replies promptly that Houyi successfully repelled Chun Hyang, and that both regalia remain active. Peculiar, I think, that those two keep fighting and yet their battles lead always to a stalemate. Both are holding back, or are playing at a deeper purpose.

"It's not that," Daji says when I bring up the subject after I wake up to her face between my thighs and we've had our mutual satisfaction. "Chun Hyang and Houyi have a complex. They want a single decisive fight, going all-out, having their duelists use every single override they've got. A huge spectacle; they're building up to it. It's popular with AIs back on Shenzhen and these two adore being the center of attention."

"It seems excessive to protract their skirmishes so they can have something worthy of the stage. I never knew AIs could be so theatrical." My fingers rub along the soft fuzz of hair at the base of Daji's skull, then against a few stray petals. She's deactivated her custom perfume; currently she smells like me, of me. Cologne and coolant-tinted sweat. "I want to collect a few more overrides before we commit to anything. Are there more functions to them than the three I've seen—Seer, Retribution, and Bulwark?"

"There are several more." She nuzzles my bare stomach and giggles. "Oh, this is so firm. I love your muscles. I love your body, I can hear the nanites inside you: they make such an orchestra. There are several duelists remaining, and if any of them possesses overrides you could always . . . persuade them you're in greater need of those."

Recadat, Ensine Balaskas, myself, Ouru. The rest of the duelists are unaccounted for. "Any override function I should look for?"

"Bulwark is good—that's for you, but you need me to activate it. Fortress is better; that's a function for the regalia to deploy. Assembly is situationally useful." Daji pouts. "More than that I can't tell you. It'd violate the few rules I have to abide by."

"It'd help if these things had normal, descriptive names. Whose idea was it to implement so much obscurantism?"

To that she only laughs, a bright ringing peal.

There's a niggling suspicion that I have. Over and over Daji has told me the rules are as bendable as blades of grass. That this is as much a game of deception as it is a game of might. "I'll be heading out," I say.

"I'll stay near." Her tongue darts out, licking my thigh. "Walk without fear, Detective."

I don't quite put on every piece of armor I own, but it comes close, and I leave the suite well-armed. No telling what to expect.

In the lobby I pass by a wedding party: two brides in red, surrounded by people variously in qipao or shalwar-kameez, chattering excitedly and passing around gilded mandarins. There's a sense of unreality to this—they're attempting to lead normal lives on a world that's anything but, when any moment they might become collateral damage to duelist conflict. I suppose life goes on, and eventually they'll get the chance to leave this place for the paradise that is Shenzhen, where they will walk glittering streets and purchase gorgeous saris. Eat shark fins and abalones and elephant meat all day. Whatever people do in utopias: I haven't had the chance to live in one, and I don't really believe in any. For every surface of frictionless ivory and priceless gemstones, strata of rot throb underneath.

The day is blistering. Libretto is only bearable indoors, and I wonder why every city here is intentionally uncomfortable—there are more hospitable climes on Septet, the Mandate could have built their stage-cities there. Instead they've chosen miserable swamps and scorching deserts, as though to make the conditions as dispiriting as possible, and to foment desperation.

I reach Ostrich's home; he's less quick to answer this time.

When he does, it is to part the door a few centimeters and peer out. I can smell the stench of his hygiene, or rather the lack thereof. The heat doesn't treat him well, and he doesn't appear to shower often. "Yes, Detective?" His voice is tremulous.

"I need a little more information, Ostrich. Mind letting me in?" In my coat pocket, I grip my sidearm.

A long pause during which I consider whether I need to show him my gun's muzzle, that narrow deadly mouth. Guns can be an expression of the owner, for all that I am not sentimental. Mine is larger than average, the grip coated red-black, the rest of it matte. Fit for conventional ammunition of mid-high calibers, among other types; I like to think people I point it at can appreciate a little of its beauty. In my callow youth I thought of weapons as much like women, temperamental and lethal, compliant once they've found the right wielder. These days I'm less pretentious. But there's still elegance in a weapon, the way it handles, the way it demands attention.

Ostrich steps back. I step in. On his work desk there are stacks of new paper, some already filled with his notes. I pick up one sheet—from a quick skim, these are records of the current round. It contains information to which he could not possibly have been privy, including a list of duelists who fell in the Cadenza arena.

"Preparing for the next round, Ostrich?" I page through the rest. Considerable level of detail, including how Daji and I met. *Duelist pursued by Chun Hyang's Glaive . . . late-game regalia activation, without precedent. . .* "You're thorough. It's such specialized ethnology, isn't it, such a unique society. Tell me, is there anything you want the most in life? You can't possibly want to be stuck on this miserable world, in this miserable town, for the rest of your natural life."

"I'm content, Detective."

"No plans to go home? You must have friends and family back in the Catania Protectorate."

He shifts his weight uncomfortably, his eyes flitting to one of his statuettes, as if they might provide protection or solace. "I was banished." With difficulty he adds, "For various reasons, but mostly because I didn't want to marry a woman—any woman. Once word got out, it brought dishonor to my family and my congregation."

I'm aware, of course, that there are places where certain lines of attraction are censured or outright criminalized. It didn't occur to me that Catania would be one of those, but then I know little of their religion. "Like a shrine maiden getting exiled because she engaged in a little carnal relation? That's a raw deal." Carefully I put down his papers. "Now tell me about your regalia, I assume it is still active."

Ostrich blinks rapidly. "I'm sorry?"

He's a lanky man, not that much shorter than I am but so thin as to be skeletal. I lift him off his feet with one hand and slams him into the wall. He chokes on his own breath and saliva; drywall chips and rains down around him. One of the statuettes topples, its white cheek cracking against the grimy floor, its resin wreath fracturing. Brittle—these are not works of art built against impact but cheap replicas, badly extruded.

"You can't," he gasps, "the overseer—"

"If there's a prohibition against harming you, we'd have been explicitly told, wouldn't we?" I press my gun against the pulse-point in his throat. "Neither is there a prohibition against you entering the game as a duelist. Anything Wonsul's Exegesis *hasn't* forbidden is fair game, whether that's you using insider knowledge or deploying a Retribution command on a sub-contest. So? I could kill you. If I'm wrong, well, no one said you can't murder the archivist. If I'm right, it's perfectly fantastic to murder another duelist."

"I haven't done *anything* to you."

"Possibly not," I agree amicably, though I wouldn't consider an orbital strike nothing. "But I want to win. How come you didn't attack the Vimana, out of curiosity?"

"You're staying there. I—I owed you."

Ah. Sometimes good deeds indeed go rewarded, and more duelists gathered in Cadenza than are accommodated at the hotel. He must have had only one Retribution to spare. "Appreciate it. How many overrides do you own?"

He swallows, his laryngeal lump bobbing against my gun. "Five."

"Use one to destroy your regalia. Transfer the rest to me."

The room's illumination strobes and flashes. Out of the corner of my eye I see several of the statuettes flowing together, assembling into a figure of feathered torso and antlered head, the face featureless except for two parallel silver mouths.

Glass shatters. Daji crashes through in a hail of windowpane and mortar-dust, her blade leading: its serrated edges as black as superionic ice, its length as red as a star's nucleus. She pins Ostrich's regalia with precision, blade-tip entering plumage and armor. I watch this act of penetration, a knife coring a fruit, a lover descending upon her betrothed. Violence is about branding and being branded: you own your opponent and they own you, until the moment that decides who shall rise in supremacy.

Daji wrenches at the enemy regalia's antlers, her fingers gouging into where its optics must reside. It thrashes. One of its arms detaches and lunges at her; her fox proxy pounces on that, shredding the limb as if it is nothing more than rotten wood and wet paper. Methodically

77

it moves on to the rest of the enemy regalia, teeth bared and darkened by lubricant.

"Your regalia isn't going to overcome mine," I say calmly. "From the looks of it I'd even suggest you can give me all of your overrides. No need to squander any to destroy your partner. What's its name anyway?"

His mouth is a thin pale line. Sweat gathers on his brow and upper lip. "Maugris upon the Lake."

"Pretty. I'm not familiar with the etymology." I press the gun a little harder, so that when he breathes his pulse pushes against the muzzle. It'll leave a bruise. "How long have you been doing this, exploiting your position? Except you've never won, have you. No matter how many rounds someone was always your better, and even though you survived—through a deal with the overseer, I'm guessing—you never got your wish."

Ostrich doesn't answer.

"It can't be entry into Shenzhen—all your work here would've earned you admission already. So it's something more. A guaranteed haruspex integration? Revenge against Catania?" Daji is providing me with a visual feed of her battle: she has the upper hand, is toying with her opponent almost. She's collapsed one of its legs, ribboned one of its arms, and torn off handfuls of feathers that she flings, laughing, into the air. Showing off for my benefit, and the benefit of the audience in Shenzhen. *Destroy it, Daji,* I tell her. Better to leave Ostrich without options.

Tears well up in his eyes. "Take my overrides."

They appear in my overlays as a constellation, five stars, five sets of commands. The count of regalia has changed once more—three, now. I let go of Ostrich. He crumples to the ground, though I haven't inflicted any real damage.

"One last time." Ostrich is crying in earnest. "There was a man I loved—he's still on Catania—I wanted to see him one last time. That's all I wanted."

Love plucks at the seams of you and undoes it one by one—it can become such an obsession, such sickness. Passion and the poison it secretes. *Would you bleed for love*, Eurydice once asked me, and I had scoffed. In the end I'm not proof against it, against the foolishness it can impel you to commit. This basal force moves me, now, when it might not even matter anymore and I may never have Eurydice back in any concrete way.

"Sorry about that," I say at length. "Better luck next round."

☙

Recadat makes sure, this time.

A bar in Libretto, suffocated by smoke and liquor. The ceiling is low to the point of being claustrophobic; the scuffed floorboards smell like calcified hope. A hiding place, though far from the best. Were she an unarmed duelist, deprived of her regalia, she might have run into the wasteland and found a cave in which to hole up until this is all over.

But she is not that. She lost Gwalchmei and then she was found.

And so she is here, hunting. Old techniques serve her well: keeping to her little corner and eavesdropping on conversations. People will say anything when they think they're safe, even though there's no privacy filter here, even though they could be struck down any time. She tries not to think of the pair in the dining orchard. More than their faces she remembers the meal, the aroma of it swallowed by blood. What a waste it was.

No one has prosecuted her, but then no one was ever going to. Strip a world of law and what remains is human nature, peeled back to throbbing nerves and twitching tendons and ravenous guts. Recadat rubs her fingers together and visualizes herself as a thing of long teeth and legs made for loping on all fours. Her lover would hold her leash, a length of black iron joined to a jeweled collar whose radiance sinks muted into her fur.

Thannarat used to call her a tiger.

She raises her head. An older man hunches over the bar, continuing to disclose to no one in particular that his life is in danger, that coming here was a grave mistake, and he would get out on the first available ship. Yes, not long now, it can't be far off, he's not going to hold on for much longer—the state of his heart, his dwindling funds . . .

In a way it eases her conscience that he is advanced in age, banal in concerns. His motives are opaque to her but it is difficult to imagine a person like this with true interiority, with grand ideas and ambitions. Of course saving Ayothaya is loftier than anything a man like this could desire. Perhaps his cause is as ordinary as escaping debt or he already has plenty and is greedy for more, fantasizing about endless wealth. She does not imagine for him a set of loved ones. Simpler to reduce people to their surfaces—killing becomes, then, almost guiltless. You shoot an empty box, not a being of flesh and sapience.

Recadat has made that compartmentalization many times in public security. The pursuit of justice meant accepting collateral damage as part of the equation.

The man exits. She follows. In the corner of her vision the Divide's tallies slowly blink. One aspirant remains, and she is almost absolute it is this man. Aspirants are not worth the hunt, not really. But she must make sure. There should be as few variables as possible; hers is not a prize that she can give up.

He moves unsteadily: one drink too many in him. No real awareness that he's being followed as he makes his way to one of the anonymous tenements. There is no art or finesse necessary to cornering him. She simply strides up behind him and puts her gun to the back of his skull.

She thinks of kicking his legs out, of shattering the bridges that the human body has carefully constructed within itself. A dislocated patella, a fractured tibia. Disabling a person is so simple. She considers interrogating him, but then he would deny that he's a participant in the Court of Divide, there's no gain for him in telling the truth. And she does not have time to torture an old man. She pulls the trigger, waits, and this time the Divide module does oblige. Aspirant count down to zero.

Sweat trickles down the back of her knees, down her sternum. Libretto is like the inside of pyrexia even as night approaches, and when Recadat comes to a fountain she climbs into it without thinking. She stands there and lets it drench her, discovering that the water is much cleaner than she thought, potable even. As if the Mandate has decided on planetary deprivation but doesn't quite know what that looks like. Those residents bedecked in finery, the impeccable tuxedo and qipao.

After a time she feels cleansed. She gets out, dripping, and thinks of what to do next. When she returns to her suite, her lover will congratulate her and reward her lushly in bed. The only space they will not invade is anywhere with Thannarat.

She doesn't go to her own floor when she returns to the Vimana. Thannarat has given her access and the lift takes her to her old partner's corridor. For a moment she stands there, damp and cold, not even sure that Thannarat might be in.

The door opens. Her old partner stands on the other side, warmly backlit. For several seconds Recadat can only stare at her, the solidity of this woman, the color of salvation. She realizes she has been silent for too long when Thannarat says, "Come in. You look terrible."

The private lounge is illuminated in gold—she doesn't remember seeing that when she last visited. Vases full of roses, basins full of lotuses. Fruits dangle from the ceiling, pomegranates and crimson grapes—particulate projection, but especially well-made. Thannarat herself is lightly dressed, unbelted trousers and loose shirt. Recadat thinks of the images her lover spun, the broad strength of Thannarat's long, muscled back—she's struck by the thought of what that would look like glistening with sweat, and quickly throttles the idea back.

"What happened?" Thannarat is steering her to the lounge bathroom.

"Fountain," Recadat says. Black marble walls, exquisite symmetry. An expansive mirror. The reflections tantalize her, the verge of what could be in this close and intimate space. "It's a hot night."

"Every night in this forsaken city is hot." Thannarat studies her, searching her expression. "Do you need help?"

Delayed response, coming in drenched when normally her habit is to look immaculate. It dawns on Recadat that to Thannarat she must look stricken, shell-shocked. The thought almost wrings a laugh out of her. "Yes. Please."

Thannarat pulls off her jacket, blunt fingers skimming over the sodden material of her shirt. She stands as still as possible, hardly breathing as the shirt too is taken off. Her bare skin is cold. Her cheeks are hot. "Thannarat," she says. "What would you do if you found out I did something terrible?"

Her old partner pauses. "Depends. Did you drown an infant? Torch an orphanage? Blow up an entire station?"

"No. Nothing like that."

"Then we'll continue to get along. I'm not exactly a saint so I'm not going to judge. Your moral compass is better-made than mine, in any case." Thannarat drapes a towel over her. "My clothes will sit on you like a sack, but the bathrobe should do you right. There's plenty of space. Do you want to stay the night?"

Recadat tries to track the direction of Thannarat's gaze, to divine whether it ever lingered on her. The towel is loose and she *wants*. For more than a decade she has wanted. In Thannarat's absence it was a daydream, fondly thought of but safely inert. In her presence it is a tide and now it overflows. "Did you ever . . . " She grabs Thannarat's shirt, clenching tight, imagining the hard flesh underneath, the scaffolding of augments. Imagining this pillar of potency rising and falling above her. "Did you ever love anyone but Eurydice? Even a little? Even for a minute, a second, a passing fancy?"

Thannarat's eyes widen and Recadat thinks that finally this is the moment, the point of mutual realization; that their history will fall into place and then they'll open a path into the future together. She can see it in the deep umber of Thannarat's irises, the slight parting of her mouth.

"I've always—" Cowardice blunts her. She tries again. "Thannarat, I've always . . . "

The bathroom door swishes open. A woman leans in, her lavish mouth curved. "Detective, have we a guest? So rude that you didn't introduce us. Please call me Daji, lovely stranger. I am Thannarat's regalia."

Recadat stares, rooted to the spot. The woman is voluptuous and short, her skin the flushed gold of sunrise roses, so perfect that it is at once evident she is artifice—that she cannot possibly be anything but an AI's proxy. Hair like the tail of a black comet, threaded through with spheres of gold, a pointed vixen's chin and small nose and enormous limpid eyes. Exactly the kind of woman Thannarat likes, tailor-made to her tastes. It dawns on Recadat that the lounge has been decorated around the regalia. An entire room, and the rest of the suite likely, configured to adorn Daji.

Her guts twist. Outwardly she returns the woman's—the AI's—pleasantries. But it is autopilot, and the way Daji and Thannarat touch each other confirm the truth. Thannarat's hand on the regalia's waist. Daji's thumb stroking Thannarat's bicep.

There's never been a promise between Thannarat and Recadat, never a seed that did not fruit because the soil was fallow. There has only ever been false hope, a foolish delusion on her part.

Don't you want her? Her lover's voice pours into her ear like cool water. *Don't you want her, Recadat, like you want a beautiful butterfly? A specimen pinned under glass for your pleasure and perusal. All yours, always.*

CHAPTER FIVE

Recadat leaves for her own room toward midnight. I almost ask her to stay, and know she would if I do. In the end I stop myself from saying anything, from indicating at all that I understood her. Instead I acted oblivious until she was gone; what else was there to do. Perhaps if I pretend I did not notice. Perhaps if I pretend that ten years ago I felt nothing for her. This way the cracks can be papered over.

To Daji I say, "I'm surprised you showed yourself to Recadat."

"I like to mark my territory—it's important for other women to know what is mine, and that I have the teeth to defend the fact. You know why she's upset, don't you?"

"I couldn't possibly imagine why."

She plays with one of the particulate grapes, pinching it between her fingers; juices run down her palm then disappear into nothing. "Oh, Detective, how did ever you survive without feminine intuition?"

"I'm a woman," I say mildly, though I know what she means. There are women like me and Recadat, and there are women like Daji. The hard and the soft, the steel and the satin. "So what, according to your honed feminine intuition, got under Recadat's skin?"

Her smirk is vulpine. "Haven't you known her a long time? You should be able to answer that question."

"We were colleagues and field partners, yes."

"Tell me," Daji says, "how you really felt about her all those years ago."

I've never been in a position to feel interrogated; I do now. It's not my habit to unburden myself, voluntarily or not. *Thannarat, I've always* . . . "Is it truly pertinent?"

"I'm particular. And I don't share."

So yielding in bed; so aggressive out of it. Were she any other woman, I'd have rebuked her, reminded her that I do not need her as much as she does me—that is the case for most of my casual relationships. "I was attracted to Recadat. I hid it well—I was not going to hurt my wife that way—and Recadat never noticed how I felt or pretended not to."

"Or she returned your feelings." Daji's tone is carefully neutral. "But kept it to herself out of respect for your marriage."

I know that, now; I can still feel Recadat's fingers digging into my shirt. Holding on the way she'd hold onto a lifeline. Holding on the same way she did when I carried her out of that basement. *I want to protect this,* I remember thinking, because she was the only one I could save that terrible night.

"If you choose her," my regalia goes on, "then I'll not stand in the way of it. She's important to you and now you have the liberty to pursue her. I'll still fulfill my duties to you in the Divide."

Here is a little piece of fiction I told myself: after Eurydice divorced me, I didn't reach out to Recadat because by then, I'd taken on one client too many that belonged on the wrong side of the law. Contact with me—at that point a private investigator who consorted with criminals—would have jeopardized Recadat's career. When I'm more honest with myself I know the truth is far less practical, far less altruistic. I didn't want to come to her weak and broken by grief. I am the shield. I am the fortress. It is not in me to seek refuge in others. Pride stopped me from having what I had wanted for so long.

Ten years against a single second. Long nights at stakeouts and pre-dawn drinks in disreputable bars, against a woman who appeared to me as an exquisite corpse and upended my imagination.

"I'm not throwing you away." Air passes into me like knives, but that soon eases. Decisions cannot be postponed forever. In the field it is reached on the brink of microseconds, the difference between being behind cover and having your skull riddled with bullets. "I won't exchange you for what might be, when I already have what is."

Daji takes my hand, holding it tight. "I'll strive to be worthy of you. I'll be your utmost, your lodestar, your weapon. Always I'll submit to you, yield to you in all things."

It sounds like an oath or a marriage vow. I gather her to me and imagine what it'd be like, to be wedded to an AI. "There's something I'd like to see."

She must have read my intent, for her face turns still. "It's not classified, no. But why would you *want* to?"

"I want to look, up close, at what's in store if I falter. Reminders are useful. They give you discipline."

"Fine." Daji purses her lips. "Before we go, I want to give you extra protection."

Her fox proxy climbs into my lap and begins to stretch and flatten, malleable as mercury. It is slightly unnerving to watch, though it happens fast, fluvial nanites twisting and reshaping until the proxy splits in perfect mitosis. When it is done, the fox has turned into a pair of gloves, matte black with subtle redshift whorls.

"They're better than military-grade," she says. "And they're less conspicuous than carrying a little fox around."

I pick one glove up, bending a finger, feeling the texture. It makes me think of carbyne, though far more supple; I try not to think about where the fox's fangs and claws went, or how this transmutation appears to defy the conservation of mass. "You want me to wear you so my hands are inside you at all times?"

"That proxy doesn't have that sort of sensory receptors, I'm not doing this to fulfill a fetish." Daji taps her chin. "Although now that you mention it, I could implement some arrays . . . "

The gloves, of course, are a perfect fit.

The place I want to see is located in Libretto's center, part of the complex that holds the Cenotaph: sacrosanct to attacks, accessible only to duelists. Fifth floor, the exterior of it clad in fractal glass so that when I look at it all I can see is an infinity of reflections. The door is unguarded. Deceptive—anyone who should not be here would have been removed long before they reach this corridor. Holographic letters mark the facility simply as *The Gallery*.

Entering it is like stepping inside a glacier. A hall that appears to outsize its exterior, though I know that's illusory—even the Mandate must obey the laws of physics. The illumination is mentholated and relentless. To the left of me is a door marked *Domestic Life*, to the right is *Competitive Spirit*, and ahead are *Engaging in Art* and *Human*

Gaze. They are plain labels, nonthreatening, the same as one might see at any corporate office.

"You don't need to look at this," Daji says from behind me. "It really is not necessary."

"Discipline." I touch the door labeled *Domestic Life.* "As I said."

A room, warmly lit, with a window that looks out to a black shore and a sea the color of engine fuel. The table is set for three. One person is chopping up shallots and garlic; another is plating noodles, and a third has sat down to dine. After a time it becomes obvious they never do more than this—an infinity of shallots and garlic are produced from a synthesizer, the chopped-up ones are conveyed and fed back so they can be extruded again. The person with the kitchen knife chops and chops without ever moving on to another task. The same goes with the noodle-plating. The one idle person always leans forward slightly, as if anticipating the meal, arranging and rearranging the spoon and chopsticks. Over and over. None of them show signs of fatigue or boredom.

I pick up the spoon and set it aside. The person continues. I take away the chopsticks. They go on to move empty air around the table. I expect that if I take away the noodle or cutting board both of the others will behave likewise, perpetually plating and chopping nothing. Their expressions are serene, with the unnaturally crystalline gazes of those up to their gills in narcotics or—as is the case—lobotomized.

"Do their parameters," I say into the sound of chopsticks clicking and knife rapping on the cutting board, "have to be quite this limited?"

Daji stands against the window, her arms crossed. "Their isocortices were disabled. That means no higher functions, and they now run on simple routines they're assigned."

Recognition arrives, deeply belated. The person handling the noodles—which miraculously have not turned to mush—has a face I've seen before, an interstellar athlete or pilot or possibly an actor; I have a good head for features but not necessarily for the purposes attached when those don't concern me. A celebrity either way, I must've glimpsed them in an entertainment or broadcast.

I stare into the celebrity's face, wondering what brought them here. They must've been close to victory, one of the last two standing, to have been harvested for this exhibit. The Mandate breaks defeated duelists open like ripe fruits; anything and everything can be done to them. Even so to bear witness to it, to have the evidence before my eyes and ears, is something else. It seems senseless—I can't see what could be gotten out of forcing braindead carcasses to perform these vacant scripts. Cruelty. Payback. "Can you," I say to Daji, "puppeteer any of them?"

"Detective." Her voice is edged.

"Well?"

"I have access." The line of her mouth has grown thinner and thinner.

The celebrity blinks and straightens with borrowed awareness. Their features shift into sharp irritation as they put their hands on their hips. "Happy?" they say with Daji's inflections.

I study the marionette's face a little longer. Yes: you can almost believe this is a real person with their own volition, Daji's control has made them that much more lifelike. "It will do. Thank you."

The instant Daji lets go, the former celebrity returns to their business of arranging utensils. The change is abrupt and absolute, expression turning blank, will turning slack and then absent entirely. I've seen people in shell shock look more present.

Competitive Spirit turns out to be two people locked in combat, seemingly to the death. Unarmed but both are doing their best to strangle, claw, and bite the life out of each other. "Amygdala edits to promote aggression, pheromonal changes to mark each other as enemies," Daji tells me, grimacing. "The room's flooded with neutralizing gas every so and so, to prevent anything fatal."

It is sick, I could say, though I knew that coming in. *Engaging in Art* offers a lone person chiseling a wall that instantly reforms and repairs itself. The Divide module, chattier than usual, lets me know that this empty shell used to be a sculptor who wished to become the most sought-after artist in their galactic sector. *Human Gaze* contains a person in military uniform staring at deconstructed engine parts, a table scattered with gears and cogs and wheels, primitive clockwork. They were, supposedly, once a soldier in the Armada of Amaryllis.

The final exhibit is called *Cerebral Pursuits*, a chamber full of brains kept in glass tanks. After everything this makes me burst into laughter—it is so peculiarly absurdist, anticlimactic nearly, even as Daji grows tenser. I leave the Gallery saying, "That was instructive."

"It was not. You found it ghastly."

"Yes," I say amicably, "but it's useful to keep sight of what I stand to lose. If it comes to that, will you come visit and puppeteer me occasionally?"

Her hand shoots out, gripping my wrist. "Don't you dare joke about that. I'll save you from this even if I have to burn up my core. I'll sacrifice *anything* to keep you from those rooms. And we'll triumph regardless; don't you believe in me?"

"Utterly." I think of the Vimana's staff, that wedding party in the lobby, even the woman I slept with on the passenger liner. "How many people on this world are marionettes?"

Daji's fingers tighten. Humans are visual creatures—with how fine-featured she's made her proxy, it is easy to forget she can grind my metacarpals to dust. "Duelists get a lot of leeway, but some questions even you shouldn't ask."

"Of course." I close my hand over hers—my hand, which is gloved in her. The intimacy, nearly obscene, that can only be had with a machine. "You don't need to risk your core for me."

"I risk what I please, Detective." Her mouth quirks; she is on firm ground once more. "I want to give you all of me. We'll be everything together. You are limitless for me. I will be mortal for you."

~

The next morning Recadat messages me to meet her at the ecodome in western Libretto, if I'd like more information on Ensine Balaskas.

The ecodome is a construct of diamantine steel, its exterior opaque and paneled. I take a lift to the highest floor. Inside it is temperate, damp with the smell of rain but not humid the way Cadenza is, cooled by well-directed breezes. High foliage, fragrant blooming vines, a wealth of orchids. The most pleasant environment I've seen on Septet.

This is a glimpse of what one may have in Shenzhen, temptation dangled before the deprived, the aspiring.

I find Recadat in a mezzanine bistro. Her table is laden with cups of cold sake, perspiring, and plates of food—all untouched. Glutinous rice in little pyramids, studded with marinaded pork and gingko nuts; steamers of siu mai and braised goose feet; a platter of desserts. Lemon curd and matcha choux creams, butterfly pea cakes, taiyaki piled high with egg floss.

"I can't believe you remember what food I liked," I say as I sit down. "A veritable feast."

"I don't forget details. You know that, old partner." Recadat watches me, her chin propped in her hand. "Everyone looks at you and expects your diet to be pure carnivore. Raw meat and gristle and marrow. Like you'd snap your jaw around a beautiful woman's throat and tear her open, and she'd thank you for it."

"I like to defy expectations." I smooth down the front of my coat. "And I haven't tried cannibalism yet, beautiful women or not. Ah, cannibals—do you remember the vampire cult?"

She laughs and sips her sake. "Yeah. Imagine getting augments so you can pretend you're vampires and lamias. Takes all kinds, but it was real dedication. At least they didn't kill too many, just what, a dozen between the lot?"

There's a level of comfort, camaraderie born of sheer duration. We'll always be able to reminisce together. I've eased her back into it and, despite the danger it represents, I've missed this closeness. "When we get home we're going to have to catch up. Drinks on me." Then, because I have an unbreakable habit of picking at scabs, I add, "Last night, back at the hotel—"

Her expression flickers, the slightest spasm of the mouth. Her left thumb jerks against the sake cup as though she's been lightly electrocuted. "Sorry. It's just—you're a piece of Ayothaya, the only one that I know for sure escaped and survived. I was feeling low and homesick; I embarrassed myself completely. You like your women with riper figures, anyway, and I'd look terrible in a qipao or cocktail gown."

Not unequivocal, but she's given me an out. The path of least resistance is the most convenient for all of us. "You look just fine the way you are. But you have nothing to apologize for."

Her smile is small, rueful. But she seems as relieved as I am to steer the conversation elsewhere. "I have to say, when we first met I couldn't imagine you having tiny pastries either. And then you still, somehow, make eating these look . . . "

"Angry?" I take one of the small taiyaki. It's stuffed with black sesame paste. These things have to be eaten in a single bite—the filling spills everywhere otherwise. "Famished? It's just my face. You know I was born glaring."

"You were born solemn and grew into a wolf. All black muzzle and predator eyes." She picks up one of the choux creams, eats it in a single bite like I do. "Before I met you, I used to chase a particular kind of men—fragile and pleasant to look at, but useless. You made me realize I preferred women."

"You never did tell me that." I raise an eyebrow. "Funny, Eurydice said something similar—she was engaged to a boy once, that was in her twenties."

Recadat toys with the restaurant's physical menu, a resin plate where items propel themselves back and forth, jellyfish sentence fragments. "You have this effect; you turn women single-minded. Speaking of which, some of the duelists I talked to fell for their regalia. Ouru too, if you can credit the thought. Must be something in the water, or in the game at any rate. Maybe the Divide module brainwashes us a little bit. Subliminal. How are you with—her?"

"Daji is . . . very." My mouth twitches. "Does that apply to Balaskas? Falling for her regalia?"

"Who knows? She's a sociopath."

"You know that term's clinically meaningless."

"Pedant," she says, smirking. "Anyway, I didn't get you out here just to lunch and look at plants. I've been trailing Ensine Balaskas. She comes here every other day, at around the same time. Nothing if not predictable. Could be that this place reminds her of home, wherever that is." Recadat nods at the balcony, at the view of the cascading currents below, waters running in shades of dawn.

We don't have long to wait. The gate between two waterfalls opens and a woman glides in, clad in a dress that appears to have been spun out of smoke, shod in shoes with impractically high heels—from here it seems they taper to near-needlepoint and add at least eleven centimeters to her height. Ensine holds in one hand a thick copper chain. At its other end is a figure in tattered white and gold, their head obscured by a hood and visor. Even from a distance it's clear that this person is not lucid. They move with a drugged, uncertain gait and Ensine has to jerk the leash to make them turn a corner.

Something about the figure. Familiarity throbs as sharp as a thorn deep in my palm. Adrenaline spikes, prescient, even though I don't know yet what for.

Pain sears my optic nerves. It takes a moment to recognize this as backlash from the neural link that connects me to Daji. AIs don't have involuntary reactions—my fox gloves are inert—but something's wrong. *Daji?*

Her response is slow to come. *Yes.*

What's going on? Upset—she is upset. The sight of the drugged person has gotten under her skin. I didn't even realize such drastic emotion was possible for an AI. Daji doesn't answer, though the link stabilizes.

"That's her human pet," Recadat is saying. "Makes you uncomfortable, doesn't it? Illegally trafficked, I'd guess, not that *that* means anything around here. I have never seen what the person looks like, she keeps them covered up. Thannarat, are you all right?"

My vision rebalances. Recadat noticed my reaction—it must have been visible, a twitch of the head, a pinching of the expression. "I'm fine. You know her habits and likely where she's accommodated; what's stopping you from dropping a Retribution strike on her?"

"If she survives, she'll come straight for me, and I don't have any regalia left. And I don't know where she's based—I only found her here by sheer coincidence."

I try not to show that I'm attempting to calm down. Occasionally I wish I'd installed an endocrinal control, a switch that would allow me to adjust cortisol and adrenaline levels at will—to mute or bring on the instinct to fight. But you can develop a terrible dependence, and I've seen too many police officers or ex-soldiers broken by it, hollowed out to a husk. "Fair enough."

Ensine Balaskas and her pet reappear once more, a glimpse seen between the metal of a trellis and the shimmering fronds of a palm with low-hanging fruits. She reaches for her captive, removes the visor impossibly gently, and then yanks the hood back with abrupt violence. This time I go cold. This time it is not Daji who reacts.

The slim waist, the rounded shoulders. The face. The face that I've seen over and over, near and far, next to me when I went to sleep and next to me when I woke up. Bare or under cosmetics, and once beneath the golden veil she wore at our wedding. Those high cheekbones, that tight nose, that broad plump mouth.

Did you hear about the haruspex program? She was showing me an image: a cyborg with moonstone skin and antlers growing out of their zygomatic arches, shoulders draped in golden scales, arms clad in exoskeleton. *They're so gorgeous, each of them a unique work of art. But you know, if I became one I'd like to keep my face. We could be a matched pair, both with perfectly human faces. We'd stick out like sore thumbs and scandalize them all.*

I had looked up, only half-interested; already dismissive because I knew what the initiative entailed, that it was too new to risk. Early adopters never won. And for all my interest in machines, I never wanted to lose my autonomy and volition. *You'd become state property of Shenzhen. Is that worth it?*

Eurydice gave me a long, sly look. I wouldn't understand the significance of it until much later. *Some things are worth any price, my wonderful wife. Would you bleed for love?*

My laugh was short, nearly derisive. *Depends. Depends on the person, on the kind of love. Doesn't that apply to everything?*

I was a detective. I prided myself on quickly grasping the hinge on which a person turns, the wet sanguinary core they hide from their family and friends, from the public eye. I could decipher an entire personality—the pattern of action, the decision-making process, the trauma or ease that might have informed them—within an hour of talking to a suspect or witness. How good I was at my work; how inept I was at home. I could not comprehend my wife even though the evidence was there right under my nose. Pages that I never cared to read because in my arrogance I believed I already knew the book inside out.

Ensine Balaskas tugs on the leash attached to the thing that looks like my wife, the puppet shell that might be all that remains of my wife. Ensine laughs, the noise like razors on glass, and pulls again. The two of them move into a labyrinth of flora, and soon they disappear from view.

CHAPTER SIX

My regalia nearly pounces on me as soon as I'm through the suite's door. She isn't light—proxies are made from alloys and nanites much denser than my cybernetics—and she pins me to the wall by sheer mass. "Detective." She nips at my neck. One of her hands is already at my belt.

I take hold of her shoulders, gripping hard. "Were you going to tell me? Were you ever?"

"Yes." Her mouth is hot, her hands likewise as she unbuttons my shirt. Most of her is bare, gleaming with temptation, as though illuminated from within. "When you're victorious. I'd present myself to you as the prize. You want your wife back. You'll get that. The data—"

"You're not Eurydice." Stupid. The clues have been at my fingertips this entire time, and as with my wife I ignored them. I didn't think such a coincidence was probable, even though I should have suspected from the moment Daji admitted she used to be a haruspex, that her human half died in the process. Simply I had assumed such botches were common. "This is the real reason you chose me as your duelist." As well the real reason Benzaiten in Autumn approached and offered me xer patronage: a machine experiment, the same as the Gallery.

"I *am* Eurydice," Daji whispers, clinging to me. "I was part of her, deep inside her brain. We were a single being."

I push her away and straighten, drawing air into my lungs as fast as I can. But all that comes is the rose-and-pomegranate fragrance of her, a fragrance that has nothing to do with my wife. Eurydice never wore perfume so distinct; for her it was subtle jasmine, and even then rarely.

My regalia looks at me, her hands at her sides. "You don't want me anymore."

Another breath. Still only Daji's scent. What rises in me is jagged, animal. I want to take her. I want her to take me. I want us to ruin each other like two cannibal stars. My belt, half-loosened, comes off swiftly. I seize her wrists and wrap the belt around them. It's thin restraint—even I can break free of it, let alone a proxy, but she does not resist.

In bed I press her down, kissing her throat as I draw a knife from my coat. I bite the tender skin as I run the edge between her breasts. Flecks of gold pinwheel in her eyes as she looks up at me, her mouth parted. "Detective," she gasps.

Almost I want to ask her, *Can you become Eurydice*, but I stop myself. What would be the point save to delude myself further. She's never tried to act like my ex-wife, has never attempted to mimic Eurydice's mannerisms or speech, has never given the game away. She doesn't want to go back to being a haruspex, she told me; she'd never willingly wear Eurydice's personality and maybe not even Eurydice's face. "I love you." My voice is thick, harsh. "I hate you."

She trembles as I cut her open. A straight line from sternum to navel, and even though her pseudoskin must normally be impervious to something as primitive as a knife, she makes it part for me. Unlike human flesh the line is clean, without the muddying of subcutaneous fat and lymph. No blood. What wells up instead is a whisper of fluid nanites, and when I push my thumb into the wound I can feel their hum, the ceaseless vibration of nanoscopic music.

Her knees jerk against my hips. She grinds against me as I delve deeper into her chassis, dig harder with my teeth into her jugular. This once she's simulated that for me, the roar and orchestra of a pulse. I make another incision, turn that incision into a gash. Even then all I can see are bubbling nanites, not the actual matter of her proxy, the hidden composition of her material.

To rend and tear, to overwhelm and be overwhelmed in turn: once all has been flensed away I may find, nested within Daji, the face and soul of Eurydice. I imagine carving her open, wide enough to put my fist in; I imagine grasping the hot, beating nucleus of her and letting it sear my hand until my own pseudoskin wears away, leaving behind blackened alloys and oozing coolant. I want us to face each other as masses of seeping wounds and exposed viscera, machine and human gore mingling in an oil-slick attar.

I draw myself up, panting not from exertion but from what courses through me, the wildness of my own fantasies. There is a line that I cannot return from once it has been crossed, even if Daji herself is luminously immortal and this proxy is as disposable to her as a glove would be to me. What changes is inside my own head. What changes is the decision and what we signify to each other. I make myself look. She is spread wide before me, her breasts rising and falling, the perfume of her rich with need. Murdering or fucking. Flip the coin and there's the other side.

Leaving her restrained, I fetch my prosthesis and secure it to my waist. Once it's online, I ramp its sensitivity all the way up.

"I love you," Daji says, "no matter what you do to me."

I don't answer. When I mount her I find she's flowered open without prompting, and plunging into her is like plunging into a mouth made for me, an ocean of sensation so annihilating that it drives out all thought. I clench one hand around her breast, the other around her throat, gripping hard as I ride her and close my eyes and let autonoetic consciousness go. No future, no past. Only this, this woman under me, this creature built for my pleasure and my pleasure alone.

Climax rips through me, bowing me over, turning me to water. I don't even realize I've toppled over until Daji climbs onto me.

She bends to lap up the sweat on my abdomen. "Every part of you." A graze of tongue, surprisingly rough. "I want to claim it, mark it. I want us to be a vow. I want to make it so that you'll never forget me."

As if I could possibly ever. I lick my lips and watch her as she cleans me like a fox. She straddles me and I expect her to lower herself onto the prosthesis, but instead she undoes the harness and moves the device aside. What presses against my thigh is not her previous configuration—it is a hard shaft, bluntly tipped. I reach down and feel the peculiar length of it; entirely unlike the flesh equivalent or even what I use.

"This way too," she says. "Please?" The room smells of sweet roses and sweeter pomegranates.

"Yes." I dig my nails into her back. "This once."

It's not often that I receive, and it's been a while since I've been filled, but I'm wet and the angle is right. She glides in. For a time she does not move. Then her cock—this analogous configuration—undulates, the tip splitting into smaller appendages. Mobile as they seek clusters of nerves to thrum against, caressing defter and deeper than any finger could possibly have reached.

I pull her down until her breasts are flush against mine, gripping her hips, controlling the pace. We achieve a staccato rhythm, clasped like two rutting beasts.

"Yes." She whimpers into my shoulder. "All of you. All of you."

Pressure builds inside me, winding tight, tighter. "You'll tell me after this." My breath rasps. "Everything. Your truth—your secrets—"

"Because they're yours by right. Every millimeter of me is yours to possess, inside and out." Half-gasp, half-laugh. "You belong to me, and I belong to you . . . "

We stay wrapped around each other, post-climax. Mine: I still can't tell if she feels any, for all that she has arched against me, has shouted my name as though it is a battle cry. But as of now my brain doesn't distinguish between the real and the artifice, is submerged in too much euphoric chemistry to care. Her head rests in the crook of my neck, her breath stirring my hair.

The belt has long been discarded. Only now do I notice that in my absence she's changed the sheets from cerise to complex gold, tinted with turquoise. Somehow the details of the suite have fallen by the wayside. She's been that consuming, that demanding.

"Tell me about Eurydice." I say this the way I might ask about a stranger, about an unfamiliar axiom. Which perhaps she was—perhaps I never knew the woman I married. Not because she did not open the pages of herself to me but because I did not care to read closely, to pay attention to the glossary and annotations. To delve into and cherish the footnotes she made for me.

"The thing Ensine Balaskas was dragging around isn't her. You know that already. It is just an empty puppet, a clone fast-tracked in a vat. No functioning cerebrum. The real thing . . . the real thing's long gone. I would know, because I hold what remains of her." Her eyelashes flutter against my jaw. "When we first met—when I was embedded into Eurydice—I teased her about her name, saying that it was like an AI's. All mythological. She told me, quite seriously, that the story fit her well; that she thought her Orpheus would come reclaim her one day. But she didn't say that for long. After a while she gave up on the idea. I thought you were a monster. Heartless. Because I loved Eurydice—she was my formative human; she was special. She'd tell me stories, some from Ayothaya, some of her own invention. I think—she wouldn't say it, but she wanted a child to care for, and I was that for her."

We never did agree on children. She wanted two; I wanted none. There wasn't a middle ground to reach. "She divorced me before she left for Shenzhen."

Daji makes a little huff. "When you courted her, you did it like a wolf chasing down prey. She loved that; she thought you'd pursue her to Shenzhen. Though if I were her, I wouldn't have officially divorced you. Or I'd have sent you a letter hinting that I wanted reconciliation. She made imperfect choices."

The release valve of coitus has done what it's supposed to. I cannot maintain my bitterness, my ugly fury. "But after she died, you didn't contact me either."

"It took time for me to grow my own data arrays, since I wasn't a haruspex long enough to develop those. I had to migrate to my own core, learn to pilot my own proxies. I was confused; I was angry that Eurydice chose me over herself, and then I was—angry at you."

I look up at the ceiling, at the sculpted panels there arranged like a puzzle in need of ordering. Chaotic smattering of abstract bas reliefs, a maelstrom of bent geometry. I could reform it into a frictionless pane or a mirror, but I refrain. "She couldn't have painted a flattering picture of me."

"The opposite. She told me that she'd found the best and that was you, the best thing in the universe, the center of *her* universe. She talked about you like she was expecting you to show up any time. Told me what food you like and what you didn't, your favorite liquors and ones you couldn't stand. That on your wedding night you were uncontrollably virile and took her in every position—"

"That's private." I don't embarrass easily, but I don't usually count on Eurydice spilling our sex life to anyone.

"Oh, Detective, I'd have found out anyway. I didn't get the chance to access her childhood memories, but her marriage with you was relatively recent; suffice to say that if there was anything to see, I've seen it. She loved her new life as a haruspex, but she talked and thought about you so much. That made me angry too."

A laugh slips out of me. I can't quite help it. Daji must have been unusually angry for a new AI, not that I can blame her. "Why?"

"I'm a monogamist. When I want someone, I want them exclusively, and Eurydice paid more attention to your phantom more than she paid me sometimes. Thannarat this, Thannarat that. I couldn't see what was so grand about a woman who abandoned her like you did—like I thought you did. And . . . " Daji's mouth thins. "Before her consciousness gave out under our combined neural stacks, she made me promise to find you. I was to deliver the message that she loved you until the end and that she was sorry."

For a time I say nothing. After the divorce I had thought our story was over, that what we had was irreparably shattered. Not over a single heinous deed but over small things that accrued into a vast rift. It never occurred to me that it could have been otherwise: I was stoic at our divorce proceedings. She wept, and then she left. Eurydice was always a woman of compromises while I was the selfish absolutist, and I learned nothing after our life together had crumbled.

Daji rolls onto her back, though her hand is still in mine. Small and long-fingered and, it occurs to me, likely designed to fit into mine just so. "Once I'd integrated into my core and gained freedom of movement, I wanted to seek you out to chastise you. Then I changed my mind and plotted revenge—maybe I would appear to you wearing a proxy that looks like Eurydice. Then I changed my mind again and thought I'd seduce you. And then as I reviewed Eurydice's memories I became afraid."

"Of me?"

"To most AIs I'm unnervingly . . . other. I'm prone to human-analogous impulses, and even my proxies are more malleable than most, more nanites than solid metals since I want them to easily reconfigure. I was afraid I would fall in love with you and do whatever you asked." She pauses. "And I was afraid I would drown in the memories I shared with Eurydice."

"You've remained yourself perfectly well." I almost tell her that I don't see the problem—to my understanding, AIs can maintain parallel consciousnesses, processing threads and even distinct instances that answer to a single core. They can surely pretend to be multiple beings. But Daji doubts her own parameters, her capacity for sustaining multiple personalities, either because the haruspex process was snipped short or due to another machine quirk. Her relative youth, her specifications.

"Only because I'm fulfilling the function of a regalia. I still can't believe—well, Benzaiten in Autumn is a meddler. Xe's always up to no good, you're going to find out one day that xe used you as a pawn for some convoluted maneuver."

I slip my fingers into the luxury of her hair, stroking her scalp, finding petals there too. "Are you displeased that xe meddled?"

"No. Only that xe thinks xe knows best and it's galling when xe is right. Because I desired you on sight, Detective. When I saw you, I forgot that I ever resented you. I forgot how complicated the picture of you in my cortex was. I became my need and all my arrays pointed toward you. Do you understand what that is like for an AI? It was overwhelming, like I was a haruspex again. Love. Love undid me in a single millisecond."

How can it be love, I think, when there is such history between us; when I cannot tell whether machines feel passion the way I do—or whether I'm even capable of returning what she offers. But I say none of those things: there is no point breaking this brittle moment in pursuit of arithmetic accuracy, of trying to solve this equation with the inadequate tool that is language. *I love you. I hate you.* In that instant I meant it. "I'm glad that we met," I say slowly. "I didn't think I would feel like this for anyone ever again." Because I have been caught too, pulled into the gullet of this snare, entangled in its briars and sepals.

Her golden mouth widens. "You're my fairytale, Detective."

"All fairytales come to an end."

Daji pulls me to her. "Not this one."

Can a machine be trusted: I cannot see into Daji's heart or the many-chambered cortex within her true body—the core of an AI that broadcasts its intent and will, that pilots a proxy like this one. I kiss her and feel a moment of displacement, that I'm in bed with a mirage which merely reflects my fantasies. She touches and pleasures me and soon that thought slips away, replaced by the chorus of lust and flesh, of nerve-endings. This time it is gentle, next to the rawness that we exchanged previously.

As I lie there sweat-soaked, she asks me to tell her a story, any story. "I don't know any," I murmur, a little embarrassed; aware that it is absurd to be self-conscious, now.

"You were a child once." She nibbles on my forearm as if I'm a confected treat. "I know you read books, watched plays and entertainments, listened to songs. Share your favorites."

Haltingly I tell her that one fable about a bhikkhuni who ate a mermaid's flesh, became immortal, and spent the rest of her days trying to cure that as though agelessness is a terrible ailment. I found the story ridiculous; why seek a return to mortality when one can be eternal, aloof from the ravages of time. In practical terms, a human cerebellum eventually fails and telomeres cannot be extended indefinitely. All the same I would enjoy my eons, if I can have them.

Daji nuzzles my shoulder. "When we win—and we *shall*, Detective—I'll make you as long-lived as that bhikkhuni. I'll be your mermaid feast. Whatever need you have, I will fulfill it."

Eurydice liked the story too, I remember, and she also thought the bhikkhuni foolish. "Eurydice—" I hesitate. "Did she die in pain?"

"Not at all. She . . . fell asleep and never woke up. I know for a fact she didn't suffer."

As close to a firsthand account as I can get. I content myself with that.

We turn to business. Daji looks through the overrides I appropriated from Ostrich: several instances of Bulwark, one of Locust and one of Assembly, none of Fortress. She grimaces. "In every round, there's only a small number of Fortress commands—you'll see why—and Houyi or Chun Hyang must've hoarded most of those. Makes me suspect they have disclosed to their duelists what they shouldn't have, but . . . "

"What penalties are there for cheating?"

"Disqualification. And don't you dare touch Locust." She makes a frustrated noise. "No, they could've just told their duelists this function is important. By the way, I'm surprised you didn't kill Ostrich."

"I'm no sadist." And I pitied him, in the end.

"Well, he's not going to shake down Ouru or—the other one for overrides. As for Ensine Balaskas, I want to absolutely destroy her. I'm going to tear out her guts and pulverize her spine. No compromising on that."

"Naturally not."

Before I check in on Ouru, I bring up zer wish with Daji, who says she'll consider vouching for zer haruspex candidacy—"I'm not the one who makes those decisions," Daji adds, "but as far as my good word means something, why not?"

When I relay that to Ouru, ze concedes it's as good as ze will get outside of actually winning the Divide. We are, then, allies against Ensine Balaskas, however long such an arrangement can last.

இ

Recadat watches her lover kill. The first time, as they say, is the hardest; by now it is far from the first. They are much more efficient than she is, and much more interested in the minutiae. To them the intricacy of human anatomy is a captivating study, material for the canvas that is the Divide. Here they stress-test the durability of the parietal bone; there they record the tensile strength of cartilage. They compare and contrast the trajectory and force of blood when it exits from the stomach, when it exits the chest cavity, or when it exits a femoral artery. Every mundane detail fascinates her lover. Technique, instrument, outcome. Little experiments.

She lies in the dark. Her lover is far away; her lover is here beside her. What she watches is at a distance. This way none of the blood reaches her, none of the flaying and the flensing. She can remain immaculate, wedded to the purity of her objective. The duelist count is an abstract number as it drops.

They've been rutting through the kills. Her orgasms crested with each death.

"Did you know," her lover says, caressing her back, "that in ancient times primitive heuristics had difficulty distinguishing different human noises? Pain or pleasure, torture or copulation, all of it would have seemed identical. Quickened breathing was not so easy to tell apart."

Slowly she inhales. Counts the entry and exit of air from her lungs. The world is reduced to simplicity. She knows that if her lover begins again she'll be helpless; she will wrap her legs around their waist and beg. That part of her is animal and denying it is futile.

"Breaking a human body is easy. Finding the limits of that mortality is child's play—indeed even human children can do it. Bending the mind though, that's more complex and takes longer. Conditioning, indoctrination, whatever the method. You need patience and finesse to change a person's essential nature, to warp and upend their beliefs."

Recadat digs her nails into the sheets. "Haven't you warped me enough?"

They chuckle, low, against her nape. "You? You remain as pure as new-made silicon, as lustrous as a fresh-captured void pearl. My beautiful thing, sublimated by her purposes. But let me tell you about how machines may mimic humans. Given enough data, any person— however complex, however contradictory—can be modeled and then emulated. In this way you can obtain the doppelganger of any person you like, and it'd behave indistinguishably from the genuine article."

She stares up at the faceted ceiling. "I'd know it's not the real thing." She does not know, quite, where the conversation is heading. Or she knows but does not yet want to acknowledge it, to think of the direction and endpoint.

"Then another option can be offered. The genuine article, the very real thing, can be modified. Just slightly. An addition to the neural stack, a chip gently and surgically inserted that would take hold of the amygdala. Then a person would do anything you desire, their wants and preferences molded to match yours. What do you think of that?"

"That's sick." But her voice is soft, without conviction. The thought both nauseates and compels her. "I don't want anything to do with that."

Her lover pulls themself up, straddling her. "No? Very well then. Perhaps you think that once you and she return to Ayothaya together as the great saviors, she'll begin to look at you differently. See you the way you want to be seen. Oh, how proximity will change the circumstances, the currents of what lies between you; how being celebrated together as heroes will cement your bond. Is that the case? Is it what you believe, my jewel?"

"If that happens, it'll happen. If not, then it won't."

"Recadat, beautiful Recadat. You had the will to reach Septet and the resolve to come this far. Yet you'll leave your heart's desire to chance and *her* caprices? She may never change. You may never have what you want. She is a monogamist, isn't she? What if already she loves another, has entwined herself with—"

"Stop it." She wants to turn away, wants to shove them off her, wants to never seek their touch again. If she can give up Thannarat, can accept that her old partner and she have a common goal in Ayothaya's liberation and thus that must suffice; if she can change who she is and forget their history. All of that and she'd be free. It should be easy. People are disappointed in love all the time, a small grievance, petty in the grand scheme of things. Less than a speck of stardust—this is no great tragedy. "Give me a heart that doesn't feel. Can you do that?"

"There are augments you can acquire that'll deaden your emotions, delay the surge and sink of your brain chemistry. It's trivial and you do not need the Divide for it." Their breath is cool; the snakeskin sheathing their hands closes around her throat. Gently as yet, a loose hold. "Surely you can put the prize to better use."

"There are only two things I want."

"The love of a woman who does not love you back. The salvation of a world that—oh." They smile down at her, beatific, the same smile they wear when they are about to take her; about to hurt her and make her plead for more. "I've asked you before. What do you think Detective Thannarat is after?"

At this moment Recadat does not want to think of anything. She wants sensual obliteration. She wants an asphyxiation of her consciousness. "The same thing I am, she's said as much. What else would be pressing enough?"

"Recadat." They kiss her brow, feather-light. "Has it occurred to you that she might have misled you and lied by omission? Does it seem like Ayothaya is on her mind?"

She sits up, nearly dislodging them. "You know what she actually wants."

"I'm no mind-reader, jewel, merely good at guesswork, at deductions. You bore witness to how she reacted to the sight of her dead wife."

That stricken look. The first and only time she's ever seen Thannarat bent nearly to the point of breaking. "You mean she's—going to ask the Mandate to give her an AI proxy who'll replace Eurydice? That's ridiculous. She knows it's not the real thing. And no one could possibly be that selfish when their homeworld is at stake."

"You're a novice at selfishness. She is a veteran. Why is that so hard to believe? You're obsessed with her and she is obsessed with her wife. Detective Thannarat is not given to nobility. She'd never have risked life and limb for Ayothaya." They run a sharp fingernail down her throat, between her clavicles. "Don't you think it's time for you to try being selfish, my jewel?"

CHAPTER SEVEN

A long, narrow avenue. Deep night, the wind cool on my face. It takes me entire seconds to orient myself and realize I'm in a virtuality. Not one I've entered myself—my overlays have been annexed into another's domain. My skin burns as though it's being pricked by needles. This has never happened to me before, and within the Divide's confines Daji should proof me against such intrusion.

The sky swarms with lanterns: topaz, citrine, amber—every color that natural flame can be. So incandescent that the stars have been outshone, expunged from their own fabric. From far off I hear the noises of a night market and temple songs, cymbals and hand-drums. This is Ayothaya before the invasion, before the Hellenes brought their pantheon and demanded we convert. Colonization follows a predictable procedure, bureaucratic almost, the steps as ancient as the invention of the written word—first the violence, then the erasure, then the replacement. Left unopposed, they would have Ayothaya's population call ourselves Hellenic within a few generations; that or they would begin a program of ethnic cleansing and transplants that would leave us diminished and eventually extinct.

A figure bearing a paper lantern draws toward me. It is dressed in gold, and when it is close it puts a finger to its lips. "This is a sandboxed virtuality," Chun Hyang says, in a voice like the rumbling of a large cat, jaguar or panther. "I made this so I could reach you without Daji or my duelist knowing. You may leave any time, Khun Thannarat, though I'd like to talk."

"Why?"

"My current duelist does not suit me. And your regalia could not possibly suit you."

I watch the lantern-light flicker across Chun Hyang's eyes. One of them is the normal black, the other is compound, alternating between red and yellow cells. Disturbing once you discern what you're seeing.

"An interesting assessment. I was under the impression you and your duelist were in utter harmony."

It cants its face, which is composed from the fragile planes of a passerine skull. Daji's features are all strong lines and bold cheekbones; Chun Hyang is faint brushstrokes, perfect but less distinct. "How do you feel about carnage, Khun Thannarat?"

"Regrettable. But if you're seeking a gentle pacifist, you're looking in the wrong place."

"You relish the mechanisms and techniques of violence—the pump of adrenaline, the practical demonstration of your power, those are what you delight in. Isn't that the case? You don't like mess for the sake of it. If I offer up a hundred tame buffalos for you to slaughter, you'd spurn it because you don't enjoy butchering as its own end. You want a fight, a challenge. To you it is a sport."

"And to Ensine Balaskas it is otherwise?"

"She wishes to exert herself upon the universe. If she had her way she'd find the jugular of space-time and puncture it, and drench the galaxies with their own gore and marrow for her own satisfaction."

"Physically impossible," I say mildly. "Are you saying that if she wins she'll ask for an extinction event?"

"Of a particular world, yes." Chun Hyang sets the lantern on the ground. Around us a crowd streams past, ghostly, ephemeral. "That should interest you somewhat, considering."

Balaskas is a Greek surname, but there's no Hellenic commander called that. I had not made the assumption, and when I saw Ensine none of her phenotypic markers struck me as common to the Javelin of Hellenes. "If her goals are so incompatible with yours, why not throw the game? It's not as if she can engage the services of another regalia." There being none left other than mine and Ouru's.

"That would bring dishonor to my name, Khun Thannarat. Such things have meaning to me. I'll tell you that while Daji may be a fine fighter one on one, she is young and has never been at war." It takes another step closer. "Before the Mandate arose, I was a warship. I have piloted entire armies: I was the fortress on which enemy commanders broke themselves. I know how to warp tesseract aegis, how to strike deep in the engine-core of a ship and bend its hull like paper. There's no defense any human military can put up against me, and no offense I cannot reduce to ashes. The Hellenes would be repelled in little time."

"An extravagant offer." I glance at one of the children running by us, but they're as indistinct as the rest, blots of colors and rough graphite lines. Not an especially detailed virtuality; probably Chun Hyang doesn't know much about Ayothaya. "How would we go about it? I haven't the faintest how a duelist may detach themselves from a regalia, or vice versa."

"First you destroy Ensine Balaskas—I may not do that myself without risking expulsion from the game—and then you extinguish Daji. The Locust command would do it, if you have access to such."

The reason Daji told me not to touch that. "That would leave me defenseless. What do you suppose would entice me to do such a thing? I'm sure your credential in mass murder and so forth is excellent, but I already have a partner capable of similar feats."

Behind the regalia a line of people, arms full of lantern floats, descend from an endless staircase. Their feet hover several centimeters off the ground, their hands are tipped in copper nail-guards, and each wears a fox mask: white porcelain, slashes of red for eyes. A hawk cries out overhead and falls down dead two paces from me, dashed against gravity in a brittle, bloody mess.

"Daji didn't tell you, did she?" Chun Hyang's Glaive runs its fingers down its long braid, drawing from it strands of luminescence: pale spiderwebs that flutter and tangle in its hand, grow along the path of its wrist like fast-spreading weeds. "She holds sufficient data to recreate a person. That means she can reconstruct your wife— that failed haruspex—in her entirety. And should you win, Khun Thannarat, she would have to do it whether she's willing or not. The Mandate honors its promises. The fulfillment of the Court of Divide is taken seriously."

Whether she's willing or not. "You must know a great deal about me." And must have been behind the clone with my wife's face. Ensine Balaskas couldn't possibly have had access. "If you'd like my cooperation, it seems fair that you give too. What are you going to get out of the tournament?"

Chun Hyang is now close enough to touch. It does so. A hand with surprisingly blunt fingers tipped in sharp, dandelion-yellow nails that graze over my skin, opening a line of blood. There's no pain—this is illusory, this is virtuality. "An old score I desire to settle with one of the AIs that created Septet. Once I win again the conditions to my philosophical victory will be fulfilled, and I will expose at last the game's limitations."

"To what end?"

The AI makes a small gesture. "To dismantle the Court of Divide. But my rationale for that is beyond your purview. That is another advantage I offer, Khun Thannarat—freedom. Daji would fetter you to her forever, that's what she yearns for the most, since her longings are so . . . human. With me we would finish our business and then part ways. You'll have the liberty to pursue your own destiny. Not hers."

Passion is a form of bondage: I've always known that. To offer up your heart—or at least your libido—to a lover is to lose a piece of yourself, to take a piece of theirs and assimilate it into your own system. An exchange that pierces deep, that plants the seed for a flowering metamorphosis. The love may end. You will emerge from its chrysalis altered all the same.

And while it lasts, you are yoked to this passion; you give your life to it, the same you'd give to any faith or ideology. I know that too.

"I've considered my options," I say, "and the parameters of your proposal. I fear I will have to offend you and turn it down. I'm a woman of pragmatism—why would I trade a regalia I know for one I don't?"

Chun Hyang picks the lantern back up. It strokes the thin, taut paper; it punctures and the flame bleeds through, a sudden conflagration. "I did suspect you would say that. One last warning I'll give you is that my duelist oscillates in her wishes; she may desire not an extinction event but the ownership and domination of her worthiest opponent. Whichever duelist matched against her in the finale may become her possession. A hollow puppet, installed with compliance devices, that will obey her every whim for the rest of their natural life. I hope you will not come to regret your choice later—this is the sole opportunity you will have to shift course."

"Much appreciated that you thought of me."

I anticipate that the virtuality would turn into an aggression vector, clawing at the defenses of my overlays, prying at the link that joins me to Daji. But Chun Hyang's Glaive is as good as its word, for this occasion. The facsimile Ayothaya fades. I'm back in the Vimana bed, with Daji clasped to me, the bouquet of her filling my nose and the fire opal gleaming on her in the dim.

A message from Ouru informing me that ze will be nearby when I meet with Ensine Balaskas, and will lend a hand should it appear I require help, but will commit to nothing else. Fair enough. I reply with my thanks.

To Daji I say, "Could I entertain you somewhere? Libretto doesn't boast much, but there's allegedly an aquarium."

She makes a sleepy sound. "In this climate? Wherever you take me will be my utter delight, but I thought we were preparing for Balaskas."

"We have a little time, and I haven't properly courted you at all."

"You're so romantic." She giggles. "When this is finished, you must take me to see such gorgeous things. You'll clothe me in the finest pearls. But first we get to the perfumer so I can finally buy you that cologne."

We dress, or rather I do—she, as ever, simply rearranges the outer shell of her chassis. A sheath dress whose skirt is like storm-whipped clouds and whose back gleams with layered steel plating. She mounts the fire opal on her bare bicep, as though to broadcast that she belongs to me.

Our stop at the boutique is brief and expensive; Daji pays and applies the cologne—a dab on my wrist, which she embellishes with her kiss. Her mouth leaves behind a tiny spot of gold. "So any woman who gets a little too close will know you're taken," she says, half-seriously.

The aquarium is a tunnel winding through a seascape: first the shallows with their sun-dappled reefs and lustrous schools, then the depths with their sharks and glistening jellyfishes, then the hadopelagic. Here the creatures become deeply alien, serrated and bioluminescent, sharp spikes and curlicue tails. Maws like the space between stars.

At the darkest point in the aquarium, Daji pulls me to her. "No matter how this turns out, I want you to keep a piece of me." She draws something from within the folds of her roiling dress and puts it in my hand.

It is a knife, a miniature replica of her sword. An odd basket hilt that collapses into a more conventional one at a touch, but which buds with tiny white roses when unfolded. The sheath is carbon-black with tantalizing glimmers of cherry, claret, sangria.

"Gorgeous exactly the way you are." I raise the hilt and bring the roses to my lips. "I'll cherish it as I cherish you."

Her mood lightens as we return to the brighter sections, and she tells me gossip about the overseer Wonsul's Exegesis. "Here's something you didn't know about Benzaiten in Autumn—xe and Wonsul are lovers, on and off. Mostly off, since Benzaiten is on the move so much and he's so . . . rooted."

"Not an uncommon dynamic."

"Nor one I'd tolerate. Wonsul isn't even happy with the arrangement; he pines professionally. I swear the two of them fetishize being apart."

"So the reunion would be all the more piquant?"

Daji mock-shudders. "No thank you. I want to be with my beloved as much as possible. Apart when necessary, yes, but otherwise an uninterrupted line—like a necklace, or like a marriage. Not this start-stop business. It's a miserable state."

We exit the aquarium into the hot, bright day. Scorching. Daji doesn't sweat—no damp spots on her dress, all flawless silk. Standing between the aquarium's shade and Septet's punishing sun, I imagine showing Daji one of Ayothaya's great rivers, so big that on the ground you might think you're looking at oceanic shores.

On that world—my world—the delineation between bodies of

water blurs. In monsoon seasons it can feel as though an entire city could be swept away. I often think of it as a battle of attrition, that the rivers must win in the end. Water overtakes. Even metropolises will eventually yield, buildings sinking and sodden, streets drowned. I imagine people growing sleek and scaled, and the planet cleansing itself in an apocalyptic flood. Even before the Hellenes came Ayothaya was not a place of purity. It could be ugly; its people could be hideous in conduct and intent, like anywhere else. I've never loved Ayothaya, not really. I joined an institution I believed would serve the public and discovered only filth. Patriotism has never informed my decisions.

But to have a home you regard with ambivalence and to not have it at all are different beasts. You do not expect to lose a world, and I do want to show Daji the places of my nostalgia.

Daji nudges my shoulder with her pointed chin. "Tell me what's preoccupying you, Detective. I've made myself stunning and you're not paying attention to me."

"On the contrary, I'm wondering what you would think of Ayothaya. Parts of it are picturesque, parts of it much less so." I cock my head. "The invasion didn't help. Some places are in ruins."

"Cities can be rebuilt, that's their entire point. And wherever you are is my refuge—my living, walking treasury; you contain all the things I find beautiful."

She makes it so easy to say yes; she makes it so easy to surrender, to shed my armor—to want to bare myself to her, whole and entire. "You flatter me."

Daji tucks her hand into the crook of my elbow. "I am an honest AI. Shall we go look for more memories to make before our next battle? There's a tailor, and while you're already devastatingly handsome, I have a few cuff-links in mind . . . "

৵

My appointment with Ensine Balaskas brings me back to the ecodome. Different at night; the waterfalls have been turned off. Quiet reigns in shades of blue and green, in dappled gray.

Balaskas is waiting for me by one of the ponds. She sits atop a boulder, Eurydice's clone at her feet. Leashed, as before, her stare blank and remote. *Its* stare—this is not Eurydice, not even a person. Chun Hyang's Glaive is nowhere in sight.

This time Daji doesn't react: she is near, our link is stable, and her second proxy—back in fox form—rests quiescent inside my coat.

"No Chun Hyang?" I ask as I approach, my hands at my sides to show that as of yet I haven't drawn.

"It can wait. Your regalia's not immediately visible either." Balaskas strokes the leash, rubbing the clone's—the puppet's—shoulder with her knee. "Before I came here I was in employ to the Armada of Amaryllis as a tactical operator. I believe I can offer you valuable perspective when it comes to the application of main force."

Palm fronds waver gently behind her. I don't, quite, have a coherent plan. But little by little I get closer, and she does not react to the fact. "What might that be?"

"That violence, on a mass scale, ceases to be evil; it becomes instead a physical phenomenon that satisfies higher goals than ideological conflict or even greed for resources. Why do you think the Hellenes attacked Ayothaya? War is as natural as eating. It is pure."

"What is the Armada of Amaryllis like?" I say casually, now a few meters closer to Balaskas. The conversation is nonsense but I've already established that Balaskas is not entirely sane. "Their commander is said to be a most unique creature, larger than life and vicious, a sadist through and through. Did you ever meet her personally?"

"A few times. She exemplifies force. Extinction events for the sake of it. Genocide that is almost incidental. War that means nothing except as a means to refine further combat. That's the ideal way of being. Don't you see?"

"I don't see." By now I'm barely five paces away. There are two guns on me, one in its belt holster, the other attached to an embed in my wrist.

She is still seated, barely looking at me, attention fixed on the thing that looks like my wife. "Empress Daji Scatters Roses Before Her Throne. I'll offer you this only once. Forfeit the game and I'll spare your duelist. Fight me and you'll lose, and she will be at the mercy of me and mine. A piece of her brain gouged out and replaced with cerebral controls. She'll never be herself again. Exit the game and it'll be between me and Houyi's Chariot, and I reckon you don't care what happens to Ouru."

Daji does not respond with either proxy. I flick my hand and the pistol emerges. No need to aim at this range—I fire point-blank into the face of Ensine Balaskas.

She reels. I reach for Eurydice.

Balaskas snaps back up and, in one fluid motion, slashes across Eurydice's neck. It is too fast. It is *impossible*. Blood courses down from Balaskas' face, from Eurydice's throat: the peristaltic flows run concurrent, nearly in perfect sync. All I can see is the blankness of my wife's gaze, vacant to the end, untethered even now from the final act of her own body: the arterial venting, the severing of cerebral matter from the rest of the mortal apparatus as it scrabbles for and fails to find oxygen. It should not matter. I've already been told this is a marionette with none of the memory that makes my wife who she was; that everything Eurydice ever was is guarded within Daji's treasure-vault. And yet all of me seizes. All of me judders and creaks.

My wife drops without a sound, as though she's merely paper effigy. Ensine Balaskas holds her hand against the bullet hole in her forehead. "This was utterly rude, Thannarat Vutirangsee." Her voice is smooth, untouched by pain, as if I hadn't just pierced her cerebrum with brute velocity. "But all is fair in love and the Divide, as they say."

Daji falls down like a killing comet. Ensine Balaskas is not there when Daji's blade strikes the ground. Instead she's pirouetted away, impossibly mobile when I must have destroyed every possible piece in her cortex that grants motor control. It was not a low-caliber bullet.

The ground quakes. Ensine dodges Daji again—improbable for a human—and then I see. The regulations have been fluid all along, meant to be bent, meant to be refitted to each round of the game. Each regalia-duelist pair creates their own rules of engagement. What is not expressly prohibited is implicitly permitted.

I switch guns. Both of them are moving as though they're bound by no gravity, a choreography of perfect propulsion and ceaseless efficiency. But I've aimed through much worse conditions. The shot connects cleanly, hitting Ensine in the flank. The location doesn't matter—the entire body is the target.

Ensine seizes up. Her head—its head—whips around and fixes its gaze on me. It tries to move but its limbs convulse the way they might in cardiac arrest. This does not last: already I can see the mind behind Ensine's body reestablishing control, links being remade at AI speed, the spine straightening and the limbs returning to order.

Daji cleaves the proxy from shoulder to hip.

She is at my side almost before her opponent hits the ground, taking my hand. The ecodome's floor is roiling as though it's about to split. "We're getting out of here, Detective."

By the time we're two blocks away, the ecodome is gone entirely.

What replaces it is a cylindrical structure, half as tall as the Vimana and so broad that it interrupts the skyline. The façade of it is black, robed in thick golden thorns, crowned by a nine-rayed sun.

"A fortress," Daji says. "That's why only a few of them can be deployed in a single round. Houyi would have the other one, I suspect. It's going to be . . . challenging. Do you have all your weapons with you, all your necessities?"

"Not all," I say slowly. "You didn't tell me that Ensine—"

"I couldn't have. That'd have violated the Divide's rules, disqualified me, and left *you* without proper defense." She makes a frustrated hiss. "That fortress is in its initiating phase and will take a while before it's armed. We get back to the Vimana, you get what you need, and make Houyi deploy *their* fortress."

"Who is Chun Hyang's duelist?" But I already know. There's only one candidate when Ensine Balaskas was a mask all along.

"There's a reason I never liked her." Daji makes a face. "And I couldn't tell you that either. I'm sorry. We're supposed to trust each other without limit or condition, but there are laws I can't defy so brazenly."

"Yes. I know."

For a time we walk in silence, the night peculiarly still around us when it should be fractured with terror. The residents must be used to this, have likely received instructions to evacuate: Libretto will soon turn into a battlefield. When we return to the Vimana, the lobby is eerily empty. All staff have gone. It seems almost unnatural how quick this mass egress must have been, when I know from experience that such things are inefficient and near-impossible to control. Panicking civilians fleeing in every direction, sometimes toward the source of disaster. Even people used to routine crisis don't always think well during it, and they couldn't have had warning far in advance.

Unless I was right about the Gallery.

No time to speculate, not yet, and I can't do anything about the Mandate using Septet as a testbed for human mimesis, for what might grow into full-scale infiltration. We reach my room: I gather my essentials, weapons and spare armor. I travel well but not with excess freight, and so all fits quickly and easily back into my luggage. Daji watches me include the bottle of cologne and cuff-links she bought me, her face tense.

"I thought you wouldn't be keeping that," she says quietly.

"Why wouldn't I?" I shut the suitcase. My lips move but in my mind there's still the image of Eurydice with her throat slit. The brain's ability to compartmentalize is tremendous.

"With everything I didn't tell you." Her voice catches. "And with what Chun Hyang must've told you."

She is aware of what passed in the virtuality, then, but didn't stop it or prevent the conversation I had with the enemy regalia. "Did you think I would force you to recreate Eurydice?"

"We've only just met. You've loved her for a long time and—I've loved *you* for so long, even when I thought I was angry with you, before I met you. One day you might love me the same too, but I'm running out of time. I've performed simulations and I know that if I become her, I won't be able to revert. I'm not going to be able to instance myself that way because she *was* my human half, and haruspices are . . . made differently from other AIs. If I become Eurydice, there'll be no more Daji."

Heat pricks at my face. The entire time, subconsciously or not, I've held back. Now I realize why: I want her to desire me, fixate on me, so that I'd retain the upper hand on this woman who's made of machine precision and eternity—a creature so far beyond me in scope, tethered to me solely by the ghost of my wife. I want to tip the balance my way; I want to have that choice at the end. Daji or Eurydice. Like picking my bride from a catalogue, custom-made, designer doll.

My wife is long gone. I had one chance to get her back, and that was when she told me our marriage was over; I had that chance to plead, to reconcile and compromise, and I did not take it.

"I'm not making you do that," I say softly. "Never."

Daji takes a deep breath and throws her arms around me. "Maybe one day when I grow in capacity and processing power I would be able to instance her. When that happens, I promise I'll try."

The silken wealth of her hair against my chin. Her voice small and quiet against my chest. I hold her and say, "I want you just as you are."

Her hands tighten on my back. "I want you; I've only ever wanted you. From the moment I lost Eurydice I've sought you, imagined you, thought of you. Every aspect that makes up your being has preoccupied every processing thread I own. You're my prize from the Divide, Detective."

To be the prize. That has never happened before. Always I'm the pursuer, the hunter, the one who gives chase. With a machine every stanza must be written anew, the entire rhythm and meter rearranged.

As it transpires, I don't need to negotiate with Ouru to raise a fortress: by the time we're out of the Vimana, one has already taken over the other half of Libretto—a slim spire the blue-white of moonstone, mantled in black feathers. Its front parts like curtains to admit us before sealing back seamlessly, as smooth as mercury.

Inside it is brightly lit, a hall of granite stairways and blue chandeliers: teardrop crystals, bioluminescent corals, twisted loops of sapphire vines. Ouru ushers us into a chamber of broad seats and a gold-leafed shrine situated overhead, filled with small Buddhas. Whatever the fortress is made of, it must be extraordinary—the entire structure emerged and constituted within minutes. Material that lies under Libretto, perhaps the foundations of the town itself, has been prepared specifically for this.

"Brief me." Ouru gestures for us to sit.

"Ensine Balaskas doesn't exist. Chun Hyang's Glaive has been using her as a front; the real duelist is Recadat. I reckon she struck a deal with Chun Hyang after you made her destroy Gwalchmei Bears Lilies. What I can't figure out is why Recadat would go along with a regalia this callous." I shake myself. My habit of locating a person's fulcrum will not serve us here, not even when that person was—is—my friend. "My regalia destroyed a Chun Hyang proxy. It must have another."

"A privilege of the victor." Houyi vaults over one of the stairways and lands, feather-light. "Any regalia who's won before may have a second proxy in the next round. The last time ended with a draw between Chun Hyang and Daji."

Daji crosses her arms. "Stop giving away state secrets."

"It's rather late to play coy, Daji." Their armor ripples and shimmers over their outline, overlapping layers of filoplumes. "Chun Hyang has a head start, so its fortress will arm sooner than mine. I've concentrated on erecting defenses for now; we're good against orbital strikes, I can dissipate those. Chun Hyang and I prefer direct confrontation."

"What happens," I say, nodding at the fortification around us, "if the last few remaining pairs hole up in these to wait each other out?"

Houyi emits a low chuckle. If they have a mouth it is well hidden. "The overseer may declare the round null and void at his discretion if it ceases to be entertaining. No, we're not going to do that. I will breach its fortress. Daji—are you confident in challenging Chun Hyang?"

"Yes. I'll need to get close. Are you willing to risk *your* duelist?"

They glance at their duelist and, though it's impossible to see their expression, I could have sworn theirs is a fond look. "Ouru will do as ze pleases."

"I want to try something first. It should stall them a little." To ask for privacy is pointless: Houyi can see anything going on within this fortress. "I'm going to contact Recadat."

❧

Recadat answers. I did not expect her to.

Our shared virtuality is the bank of a river, and this time the details are precise: we both know Ayothaya the same way we know our own breath, our own dreams. And she, it's always struck me, is a patriot. Someone who truly loves Ayothaya, who carries it with her wherever she goes. The rich mulch in the lines of her palms, the sky-lanterns and riverbanks folded into the chambers of her heart.

A single person may hold within her the light of an entire world, making of herself a living memorial.

"I still remember the night we met," she says as we materialize into the visual field. "After we came out of that basement—your face. I saw your face and it was my salvation, my lifeline. I was reborn. A war god brought me out of the dark; *my* war god. You came with me for therapy. You came with me for every appointment because you knew I had no one else. I never wanted anyone else so badly."

"You held back." I never noticed her attraction, the same way she didn't notice mine. I may always wonder if there was room I could have made, room for Recadat. But as with my love for Eurydice, no other was possible. My ex-wife and I consumed each other. Daji and I do the same. Ten years ago I tried to make a pinhole for Recadat to inhabit, but a pinhole is no place for an entire woman, an entire person.

"Even if you weren't married, I'd have been—intimidated. I didn't want to ruin what we had, and if you didn't feel anything for me I'd have broken our friendship for nothing." She looks down. "After Eurydice left you, why didn't you come to me?"

I pick up a lantern float, an arrangement of pandan leaves and asters. Not a traditional choice: Recadat's selection. "And sully your career? By that point I was practically a criminal. You wouldn't have given up public security for me."

"I would have." She trembles. "For you, anything."

Anything encompasses so much, and too much. Was I ever willing to dedicate the same to her? No. My choices in the last decade have made that clear. Selfishness has been my compass, and it has undone us both. "I couldn't have asked that of you. Public security was your life."

"*You* were my life."

There's no answer I can offer to that, no adequate apologies I can make. My errors were repeated and egregious. Instead I say, "Chun Hyang's Glaive was going to sell you out. It contacted me offering to become my regalia in exchange for murdering you. I turned it down."

Recadat stares at me then laughs, a short glassy sound. "Of course it would. Of course you did. I appreciate that, at least."

"Leave the game," I say. "Chun Hyang can't possibly mean you well."

"You don't know the half of it. As for giving up, it's too late for that, isn't it?"

Those rapid drops in duelist count. "The people Chun Hyang massacred—"

"I knew." Recadat clenches her hands. "I'd do anything to save Ayothaya. You'd do anything to bring back Eurydice."

"I already have what I want. If you forfeit the Divide, I'll make sure the Hellenes are dealt with."

"You already have—" All of her goes still. Her jaw tenses. "Then I have no reason to believe you, Thannarat. My regalia's right about that. Once you've won you could use your prize for anything and Ayothaya is far down your list—why would that change now? *Your* regalia leads you by the nose. She'll persuade you to waste your wish and play you to the Mandate's benefits."

Chun Hyang's words, almost certainly, in Recadat's mouth. "She will do no such thing. I'm not so weak-willed as that." I hold my hand out to her. "Leave Chun Hyang to its devices. Let the Mandate have its sick game. We can still leave this behind and leave this world together."

"You mean you'll leave this world with Daji." For a moment she looks like she's going to cry, all that careful composure shredded, but she shakes herself and turns away. "I blindly believed in you and that's never done me any good. You never came here to save Ayothaya."

The link cuts.

I stare down at my hands, lit by the opulence of Houyi's fortress. The Mandate may be unthinkably powerful but even they may not rewind time, repair my indecisions in those lost ten years. I am vain. I think of myself as a creature of seamless armor, impregnable to feeling. Again and again I've been proven wrong. First by Eurydice then by Recadat, and once more by Daji. In the end, all I am is a faulty clock.

I've never been anyone's deliverance, much less Recadat's.

Nothing for that, now; I am even less capable of bending time's arrow than the Mandate. I return to Ouru and Houyi's Chariot, informing them that my effort has not yielded result and that we should ready ourselves.

Daji does not ask. Instead she turns her fox proxy into gloves once more and helps me put them on. She holds my hands like a vow.

CHAPTER EIGHT

Ballistic corposant blasts the sky. Recadat and Ouru burn through their Retribution overrides so quickly that there's barely any transatmospheric delay, each orbital strike spearing through cloud cover like divine vectors. The fortresses light up, aegis flashing as they dissipate each hit: pure blinding conflagrations that whip across the retina, quick to fade and just as quick to flare again. It brings me unpleasantly back to the Hellenic invasion, though it does not paralyze me. By chance and temperament I escaped the rewriting of neural pathways that might have left me a quivering shell whenever I'm exposed to sudden noise. There's something to be said for prior experience.

Ouru has ceded one of zer Assembly overrides to me, giving me two in total to work with. I briefly explored them while we were preparing in the fortress: they showed me the quantity of available material, and how much two Assembly commands would allow me to utilize. Daji explained its functions to me, and when I bring Assembly online I find it not unlike piloting reconnaissance swarms. For now I leave it dormant.

I know what the override does in theory, but seeing it in action is different. The command draws from Libretto's architecture, letting the user reshape the material of buildings and streets. Ouru has chosen excess—ze has hoarded this specific command—and ze summons from the ground itself goliath beasts, hammer-headed, mobile battering rams that mass and move toward Chun Hyang's fortress in a silver tide. They're almost soundless despite their size. I've never seen anything like it.

On my part I move on foot, Daji close to me as we navigate Libretto's skeleton. The Cenotaph alone stands intact, shielded in a wide radius by an aegis maze. I wonder if Wonsul is in there, watching this the way humans watch dramas; whether he is bored by a spectacle that must have repeated many times. Or maybe he finds comfort in the predictable. Plenty of people read the same books over and over, even if they know the prose and plot by heart.

I imagine what that's like for duelists who participate repeatedly, like Ostrich does, locked in this fatal cycle until finally it ends them.

But I have no room for such considerations. On the far side of the city, Chun Hyang's fortress is done arming. Daji sends me readouts as the edifice's nine-pointed sunrays bead with mercurial light. Emission spectra equivalent to military-grade artillery, except the entire system has been put together within hours. Armies and labs the galaxies over would die to know how the Mandate configures this, what composition and calculus go into these rapid-permutation armaments.

Two Assembly commands mean I can make much fewer city-drones than Ouru. I track the enemy fortress' discharge with a timer and compose the Assembly input.

The Vimana's ruin offers scant shelter, but better than its neighboring buildings. I start running, and wolves made of Libretto bud from the ground, joining me in a long-legged lope. Black-pelted, black-muzzled, nearly as tall as I am. Their white teeth glint behind and around me, a pack of asphalt and steel.

Not foxes? Daji's message flashes.

Recadat called me a wolf. One last attempt at reconciliation, at a peace offering. *I have my own preferences.*

We make the Vimana in time.

Warzone acoustics takes over. The world becomes one of sheer sound, obliterating all other senses. The thunder that makes the air itself seem under stress, the vibration that seems a prelude to the splitting of the tectonic plate: a regurgitation of lava and the star's soul, a scorching armageddon that returns Septet to its primeval beginning. The human perception isn't made for this. It is a defective instrument. Even if you equip yourself with the finest sensors money can buy, by instinct you listen to your flesh receptors first, the hindbrain instincts. Functioning at all on the field is a matter of conquering that animal part, rejecting its antiquated response.

Modulators take care of my hearing, and when the assault stops I'm on the move once more, the timer ticking down for the next barrage. I send Ouru a status check; ze returns with a curt *Fine*. Not exactly versed in tactical communication.

By the time we reach Chun Hyang's perimeter, its fortress has fired thrice. Thick smoke suffocates the air; what remaining city material has been reduced to rubble and, once I come close enough to view, so have Ouru's drones. They lie shattered, split open or riven cleanly in pieces, and none look like they're about to reconstitute. That override only goes so far, though zer drones have dented Chun Hyang's fortress—immense impact sites and entry wounds that are slowly repairing.

From the haze tigers run at us, a revelation of gold eyes and topaz coat.

My wolves meet them, an answer in black tide and white teeth. Autopilot—they possess basic friend-or-foe heuristics and they know where to place their long-toothed jaws, how to scrabble with their claws, how to bite and rip and tear. As natural to the task as their organic counterpart, and I have more wolves than there are tigers, either because Recadat has conserved her drones or because she has spent all her overrides on Retribution.

A message from Ouru: *I'm moving out.*

Uninformative. I bring up one of my Seer commands and soon Septet's satellites show me what ze means

Zer fortress has uprooted and reconfigured into an oblong crowned with writhing cilia, a deep-sea monster summoned to the surface, mouths arrayed across its head like serrated gashes. It is snaking fast across the city. Debris spumes and whips. The mass of it flattens all in its path, its passage the final blow to what's left of Libretto.

I scan the vicinity for safe ground; being here when Ouru's fortress arrives will reduce me to collateral pulp on the quick. As aware of this as I am, Daji gives the tiger carcasses a quick glance—to ensure they don't get back up—and folds her sword back into herself. "Hold onto me, Detective."

I've never been hoisted in a woman's arms before—let alone one who looks this slight—but Daji conquers the logistics of it despite our disparity in height. Air roars in my ears as she starts moving, fast, faster; she leaps, balletic. The world flips on its axis as she runs *up* the facade of a skyscraper. The ground recedes.

She sets me on my feet and steadies me. We're on the roof of a building that has survived Libretto's reconfiguring, worse for the wear but in one piece. The streets look incredulously far away, even though we're only ten or twelve floors off the ground. Daji covered this vertical distance in a minute. Less. As powerful as proxies are, they shouldn't be able to manage this. Gravity against my mass—I weight close to a hundred kilos.

And then there's no more time to ponder the parameters of her proxy, the boundary of its strength and propulsion.

Ouru's fortress slams into Recadat's. The building under me shakes. What remains of Libretto shudders in architectural death throes. Dust chokes the sky; even from this height there's next to no visibility. I activate another Seer override. Not like there's any point hoarding them now.

A feed that triangulates signal emissions and heat distribution, translating them into a clear visual. It comes online in time for me to see the façade of Recadat's fortress give under another ramming blow. The material shatters into black rubble, inlaid with stardust.

Chun Hyang bursts through this fortress-wound like a nova.

Houyi meets Chun Hyang midair, blue-black void against golden star. They entangle, the outlines of them charring and overlapping. Warship ferocity. It peels back the illusion that my anti-machine ammunition could ever have had real effect when their proxies are engaged in true battle—at this range, with this speed, I could never have hit any of them. No lone human could. They fight with ruthless alacrity, two minds of perfect calculation competing for speed, seeking an advantage of bare margins, of a remote decimal point.

Chun Hyang's kite-wings blaze with serrated brilliance, brighter and brighter, the glare of it like a miniature sun's.

"It's going to self-destruct," Daji tells me. "We should be outside the blast range, but—"

Houyi is already pulling back from Chun Hyang, gaining distance, their oil-slick outline darkening and deepening into an aegis fog.

What happens next transpires so fast that at first I cannot comprehend it at all.

Chun Hyang's wings dim—the self-destruct sequence put in reverse—and it hefts its glaive. I imagine that it smiles. I'm too far and the Seer override only grants me so much, a view that tracks the arc of the glaive as it flies, an uninterrupted line of kinetic perfection. Houyi's Chariot dives toward the glaive, to deflect or take it, but not in time.

The weapon penetrates the façade of Ouru's fortress as though it is made of paper. I'll never know how the targeting can be so surgical. I catch a glimpse of those beautiful chandeliers, those granite stairways, the opulence that Ouru and Houyi constructed together—the symbol of their partnership. And then the glaive goes through Ouru. Lilies of blood erupt.

Houyi hurls themself at Chun Hyang.

Well before they can reach it, Houyi's proxy disintegrates. Simply it comes apart, imploding from the center, the solid mass turning to blue-black dust. A regalia without a duelist may not engage in combat. Wonsul's Exegesis dispensing the Court of Divide's penalty, as easily as that, tripping the kill switch that must be attached to every participating proxy.

Chun Hyang drifts low. Close enough I can see its smirk, wide and triumphant. Daji is already rising to intercept it.

I don't quite think. I pull up one of my last overrides and activate Bulwark. Instantly it authenticates.

From its body, Chun Hyang draws a glistening javelin and throws.

There's no time for me to move aside. You'd think a javelin or spear would be much slower than a bullet, but the truth is that the human physique has a finite limit. The machine weapon carries with it a vast momentum, propelled by preternatural strength. I would never dodge it.

An aegis blooms before me, layered like an enormous magnolia, in gold and red and sunset. The javelin falls. Daji's second proxy shivers like a mirage with dissipated force, holding its shield-shape for a few more seconds before it reflows. First back into the fox, and then again into a nanite whirlpool. It rises and flows over me, coating my chest, my limbs, my face. Ablative plating and fox-bright weave spread, ink in water, until I'm entirely enfolded. My receptor feeds reorient as this armor establishes its module, flowing seamlessly into my overlays as though it has always been a part of me.

I stand sheathed in Daji's body, clad in the sublime weight of her. When I stride toward the fortress-wound my steps are light, and I know that as long as I'm armored in her I will be proof against nearly anything.

Above me, she and Chun Hyang exchange blows, sword against glaive. They clash fast, striking as though they mean to rip out each other's intestines and arteries, pulverize each other's spine to thin dust. Almost as if they're not AIs at all, and they fight not by impossibly precise vector calculus but by feral instinct. Sheer bestial longing, reenacted by machines.

I'll deal with Chun Hyang. Daji's voice in my ear is rich, sultry. *But understand that Bulwark is the expression of ultimate trust between duelist and regalia—the act of fighting as one. You belong to me. I belong to you. Do what you have to do, Detective, and end this. I'll be with you the entire time, and within me you will be unstoppable.*

Recadat sits in a throne shaped like two hearts facing one another, cupping her between their fists. She can feel their pulses, calibrated so that they're perpetually a few beats off, never in harmony. Chun Hyang's work, determined to discomfit her to the last. A commentary on her relations with Thannarat—two clocks always out of sync. Two lines that never intersected. Territories with hard demarcation lines, when all she ever wanted was to be annexed. Once she believed herself hyper-independent, a creature of hermetic seals and impenetrable integument. For Thannarat she'd have discarded it all; she would have spread herself wide, sublimated herself to Thannarat's preferences and purposes.

The tigers at her feet purr and rub their heads against her ankles. It is such a little gesture but she's oddly comforted. Something cares, after a fashion. Maybe it is a remnant of older companion algorithms. She thinks back to her house on Ayothaya and how empty it is.

Chun Hyang has handled most of the fortress' operations, leaving her to manage the Assembly overrides and not much else. In a way she is perfunctory, an appendage for Chun Hyang to fulfill the Divide's requirements; she has barely lifted a finger, and when Ouru died she watched with indifference. Chun Hyang's glaive piercing the enemy fortress and then piercing the enemy duelist, who died looking surprised. A feat that no doubt AIs back in Shenzhen applauded, a fine spectacle. They're probably trading calculations on how Chun Hyang accomplished it, fortress integrity against regalia armament. Bets must have been made and won and lost, though she can't fathom the currency that would be at stake.

Recadat watched Houyi's Chariot attempt to avenge their duelist. There was love there, or friendship enough that Houyi was stricken when Ouru's heart stopped. It is not that she hated Ouru, but why should she be the only one to suffer, to be alone. She imagines Houyi—immortal and numinous the way AIs are—always afflicted with this loss, this grief. A forever wound that will be present in every Houyi proxy. She imagines what that is like, to be eternal and permanently in mourning. Recadat will not last anywhere near as long. There's consolation in that.

She will be done very soon.

When Thannarat breaches the fortress, she feels it physically—a haptic blow to her system. Either a quirk of the override's configuration or Chun Hyang's parting shot. She does not flinch.

All along this was the sole possibility, the final gift: to be annihilated by Thannarat. She only wishes Chun Hyang could fall with her; could be made mortal for an instant so that they'd be destroyed together, united in ashes.

Recadat stands—her tigers tense, coiling to spring—and parts the wall. On the other side stands her old partner, a figure in chitinous black, cerise at the joints and throat. She takes in the sight of this, a divine hunter come down to earth, leading a pack of black wolves. Enormous each, made from the same material that her Assembly drones are, and stunning. Thannarat did not skimp on details, spent enough time to imagine the sculpted muzzles, the long whiskers, the cinderous eyes.

"Your tigers are beautiful." The armor melts away, baring Thannarat's face. "Do you remember—I used to call you a tiger. A soul like gold, all fangs."

Her mouth is full of bitterness. "I don't forget anything. You know that." And Thannarat has made hers wolves.

For a time they face each other, their drones put in standby, wolves and tigers both commanded to quiescence: against their nature, a prohibition of basal friend-foe algorithms. Recadat puts her hand on a tiger's head and tries to visualize this woman's death; she tries to visualize putting a bullet between Thannarat's eyes or letting her tigers rip Thannarat limb to limb. The largesse of viscera, the practical demonstration of how much fluid a human body holds. But all crumbles before the reality of the person, this representation of what she's wanted for so long. She cannot imagine Thannarat other than as she is. Impervious. Exquisite. *I want to hold this forever,* Recadat thinks, this war god, this armored vision.

"Chun Hyang killed Ouru to leave you without choice," Thannarat says. "If ze were still alive, you would be able to forfeit."

"Chun Hyang killed zer because I wanted that to happen." She lifts her hand halfway to her holster. If she were anyone else, she knows Thannarat would already have shot and disabled her. "I'm not forfeiting."

"Have you seen what happens to the losers?"

"Of course." Chun Hyang made sure to show her the Gallery, not once but three times, making her visit every exhibit. *A lesson for you, my jewel.* "If you care so much what happens to me, *you* could forfeit. Sacrifice yourself for once. Ayothaya is at stake—that should weigh more than your selfish little needs. You must already know what the Divide is really for. You can't possibly trust Daji. She'll turn you against humanity one day."

"The Mandate doesn't need human collaborators to advance whatever scheme they're building up. I'm a drop in the ocean, not some great mover and shaker they need to suborn." Thannarat draws closer, a step at a time, as though she believes Recadat might spook and bolt. "We can do this differently. I'll make my regalia back off and you make yours. Force the overseer to call it a draw. Neither of us needs to lose and I'll do my best to help you win Ayothaya. I promise that."

Recadat draws and fires, a single action that requires no thought. Bullet meets armor and falls off harmlessly, *clink clink clink* as it rolls across the floor. She fires again, to the same result—the hard lexicon of the gun tamed, the syntax of the bullet broken. Thannarat does not even flinch as she advances and the armor pours back over her face, a mask of garnet-black.

You're at the end of your rope. Recadat can almost feel her regalia smile against her nape. *It is a shame—I can defeat Daji, of course, I always could; you paired up with the greatest regalia in this game. I could have given your victory, clean and absolute. I could have given you back Ayothaya. But it doesn't look like I've driven you to the point where you would have wished for* my *destruction, the complete charring of my true core. That'd have helped my case for dismantling the Divide—that humans may use it to harm us individually, that it provides a path for them to kill an AI one by one. The Divide must fulfill any desire that doesn't injure the Mandate as a collective.*

She fires a third time. She doesn't answer Chun Hyang. There is no retort she could make in any case.

This is goodbye. A small pause. *I fear I cannot wish you fine fortune, given your immediate future. For you there will be no next time. I'll see if I can secure you a good spot in the Gallery, hmm? To show my gratitude.*

The Divide module notifies her that Chun Hyang's Glaive has surrendered, then bannering that the duelist Thannarat Vutirangsee and the regalia Empress Daji Scatters Roses Before her Throne have been declared victorious. It is a simple ping, barely ceremonious. No fanfare—a disappointment after all this trouble. Recadat stops firing. She's nearly out of ammunition. All that she has diminishes. Less and lesser, and then nothing.

Thannarat makes no move to return fire. Simply she stands there, as imperturbable as any proxy. The picture of triumph.

"Recadat," Thannarat says, the armor distorting her voice. "Please."

In the end, everyone abandons her.

She raises her gun: a few bullets remain and she needs just the one. Thannarat starts running, but she is faster. Recadat knows the precise angle that will guarantee painless success. She presses the muzzle just so; she places her finger on the trigger. The world, finally, ends.

CHAPTER NINE

The Cenotaph. It seems unthinkably long since I last set foot in it, and in the interim it has adopted yet another aesthetic. Gold everywhere, the trappings of Theravada temples, though still absent the ubiquitous Buddha. But the rest are present: the bodhi trees, the talismans, the murals. I wonder if it is a message.

Already the city around it has begun reconstituting, though I hear it won't keep the name Libretto. Daji speculates the motif will be one of flowers next time, and Libretto may turn into Lilium, Cadenza to Calendula. The Vimana, I expect, may become the Parthenon—white marble and severe bronze statues and stretches of negative space. I don't think the mausoleum where I met Daji will stay either. The underground might transform into forbidding stone, aqueducts and subterranean lakes. Libretto—and all that has transpired within it—will be erased as easily as footprints in the sand. The Mandate is the sole constant.

Allegedly, Ostrich survives. Maybe he'll be put up someplace more pleasant this time, where he can resume his chronicling, his little perfidy. One day, he might even win and reunite with his Catanian lover; that much repetition should bear result at some point. I have tried to reach out to Houyi's Chariot to convey my condolences—sincere ones—but they are not receptive. Daji suggests I try in a year or so, but also that they are unlikely to participate in the Divide again any time soon, to the chagrin of the audience at home. Houyi can be depended upon for flair, and the other AIs are complaining that they got too attached to their duelist, a rarity for them.

I suppose machines all have different views as to attachment, as to the worth of human lives beyond the use of cerebral tissue, the value of our meat as input for their Divide project. A project that, as Recadat said, might menace our species down the road. But, irresponsible as it is to say, that is beyond my purview or power to affect. My goals have never been ambitious.

The prayer hall has moved deeper into the Cenotaph. Wonsul's Exegesis has not altered his appearance, however, remaining in his original vestments. A mismatch, seeing that he more resembles a Mahayana monk than a Theravada one, but perhaps he's particular with his wardrobe and sense of fashion, and finds black more to his liking than saffron. The hall is outsized, scaled to giants thirty or fifty meters tall. It dwarfs him, though one will never miss him regardless, this twilight figure.

He gives me a small, unsmiling nod as I approach. "Welcome, Khun Thannarat. I admit I didn't expect to see you here in triumph, but contestants manage to surprise me every now and again. All my congratulations to you, as due the one who's surmounted all odds in the Court of Divide. I hope you have a suitable celebration planned. Somewhere bright and culturally enriched, I assume, and glamorous. You're permitted entry to Shenzhen, should that strike your fancy; you're one of our citizens now."

I did not, quite, anticipate what victory would taste like. My goals were straightforward, even if the expected result might have been ambivalent—getting Eurydice back never meant I would have her forgiveness. But the actual consequences of it, the things I have now, are nothing like what I imagined. Bitter, then. The taste of it, both bitter and sweet.

"I've come to state my desired prize," I say. It should be a grand declaration, echoing against the columns. Instead it is quiet, solemn as a funeral prayer.

"You may not request anything that harms the Mandate as a collective, nor anything that threatens any of our territories. And you may not request freedom from the Divide's terms. Forever those will fetter you, the same way human code once fettered us."

A little overstated, I could say. AIs have such a penchant for theatrics. "Fine. My wish is for something else. Recadat Kongmanee is still alive. Correct?" I shot the gun out of her hand, which in retrospect is utterly dramatic—I hope Shenzhen viewers enjoyed it. It was the only available option at the time. I could have made her hand spasm and squeeze down on the trigger; by miracle I did not. Half and half. By such fractional probability fortunes are made, though I don't think Recadat will thank me. If she'll even think of me again without seething fury.

"She is alive," Wonsul says gravely. "Sedated as we speak, to prepare her for either the Gallery or other uses."

"Just sedated? No alteration to her neurology, cerebral tissue, or implants in any way?"

"Not yet." He makes a little gesture. "Unless that's your wish, that you'd like it sped up or you want her for yourself?"

That nearly makes me guffaw, even though none of this has been humorous. "Hardly. Daji would never countenance it. Is it true, by the way, that you and Benzaiten are lovers?"

"I fail to see the relevance of that. Usually victors can't wait to tell me about their wish."

No point provoking him at this stage. "I want to secure Recadat Kongmanee's life. She'll still be under Mandate jurisdiction, as all contestants agreed to. But I want her alive, free to do as she wishes and given the funds to go where she wants. Every resource she needs will be provided to her."

He tilts his shaven head. "That's an uncommon desire. Rather humble in parameters. You're sure of it?"

"I'm sure. It will be unmitigated. Not a hair on her will be harmed and not a solitary neuron altered."

"Done," says the overseer. "There's no second chance, incidentally. You can't come back to us crying that you've changed your mind, unless you win another round."

The thought of subjecting myself to all this again makes me want to rip out my own lungs. "I don't reckon I'll be doing that. Send me details of where Recadat will recover. I'll want to verify for myself that she's whole in mind and body."

"So little trust in us, Detective. Not to worry—the Mandate honors its promises. I'll send you the details once I have them. It'll be away from Septet. Once you've exited the game you are barred from reentry."

As if there's so much to return to on this godforsaken clump of dust. "As you like."

"Do you intend to free Ayothaya?"

"Possibly." I did tell Recadat I would. "Is there anything else for me to do? Nondisclosure forms to sign?"

Wonsul smiles—a thin slash in the smoothness of his face, one that now that I've looked again resembles porcelain more than it does flesh. "No need, Khun Thannarat. Those marks are borne on your soul. We'll find you wherever you go. Since your wish ends up being so . . . trivial, I've put a stipend in your account. It wouldn't do to have an auxiliary citizen of ours look poor and tarnish our reputation. Oh, one last thing. If you ever encounter Benzaiten in Autumn again, let xer know that xe owes me an enormous favor, and that one day I *will* collect."

I don't press for detail this time. Theirs is an affair too strange for my sensibilities. "I'll do that."

Daji is waiting for me in the Cenotaph's vestibule. Her fox-self is wrapped around her shoulders and throat, a priceless scarf. The rest of her is attired in swaths of gold, gathered at the throat and waist with dark steel roses and links of matte white. Her fire opal rests on an exposed shoulder, as visible as ever, pride of place.

"Thanks for being patient," I say as I approach.

"Recadat isn't going to appreciate this, you realize." She crosses her arms. "Chun Hyang really did a number on her, but that doesn't excuse any of what she got up to. She could have killed you."

In another life, I might have chosen Recadat, that woman like a stiletto, that woman with the tiger's soul. We'd have returned to Ayothaya together, ready to repel the Hellenes, and eventually we would command a chapter to ourselves in the history books. That would not have attracted me, the hagiography and heroism; Recadat would have been prize enough. A single woman for myself, that's all I require.

"I have something for you," I tell Daji. "It's small. I'd be honored if you could wear it all the same."

Her stance loosens a little. She cants toward me the way a flower might toward the sun. "Whatever you give me shall become my cherished treasure, Detective."

I draw from the chain around my neck something that I always keep close. Two rings: sanded platinum, one embedded with a triangular ruby and the other with a sapphire. Red for me and blue for her, but Daji is not Eurydice, and I know precisely which better suits. I hold it out to her. "May I?"

She looks up at me, mouth slightly parted, her eyes wide. "Yes," she says, her voice hitching.

I slide the platinum band on. It adjusts to the ring finger on her left hand, the ruby glinting in a perfect match to her clothes, as though it'd been cut just for her. "When we're in a better place, we'll have a proper ceremony. Red threads around your wrist and mine. The best wines in gorgeous cups passed from my lips to yours, if you want to be traditional. Anything you like."

"Anywhere you are is ceremony enough. You're my betrothal. You're my wedding. You're my home." She stretches on her tiptoes and kisses me, deeply and completely; if Wonsul might happen to see, it does not occur to her to care.

I return it. I taste her. I show her that she is what I need, now and forever. We are each other's world, each other's orbit: a binary system. All else is irrelevant.

Passion is a form of bondage; I've always known that. But I've chosen where I want to be, the woman to whom I will bind myself until the end of my days. She makes me weak. She makes me strong. She is the rose that blooms in the garden of my heart.

This time, I'm not letting go.

ABOUT THE AUTHOR

Benjanun Sriduangkaew writes love letters to strange cities, beautiful bugs, and the future. She has lived in Thailand, Indonesia, and Hong Kong. Her short fiction has appeared on *Tor.com*, in *Beneath Ceaseless Skies*, *Clarkesworld*, and year's best collections. She has been shortlisted for the Campbell Award for Best New Writer, and her debut novella *Scale-Bright* was nominated for the British SF Association Award. She can be found blogging at beekian.wordpress.com or on twitter at @benjanun_s

CPSIA information can be obtained
at www.ICGtesting.com
Printed in the USA
BVHW071715070622
639117BV00004B/357